« Hot Metal »

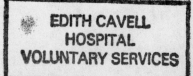

« Hot Metal »

based on the television stories

MANNA FROM HEAVEN

and

HOT METAL

Liz Holliday

First published in Great Britain in 1996 by
Virgin Books
an imprint of Virgin Publishing Ltd
332 Ladbroke Grove
London W10 5AH

BUGS the television series is produced by
Carnival Films Ltd and broadcast in the UK by BBC1

ISBN 0 753 50001 9

Typeset by Galleon Typesetting, Ipswich
Printed and bound in Great Britain by
BPC Paperbacks Ltd, Aylesbury

For Dave Renton and Martin Weaver: see – it's amazing what you get when you ask for it . . .

And, of course, for Charlie Stross – because if he hadn't existed, we'd have had to invent him.

ACKNOWLEDGEMENTS

With many thanks to Peter Darvill-Evans for having more patience than I thought humanly possible; to my agent Robert Kirby; to Andy Lane (as ever!); Barbara Morris and Martin Weaver for listening to me whinge; to Alex Stewart for being a shoulder when I needed one and an invaluable source of last minute inspiration; to Andy Lane (again), Gus Smith, Tina Anghelatos, Chris Amies, Ben Jeapes and Molly Brown for not letting me get away with too much; and to my fellow roadtrippers: Pommy Ryan, Jim Lewczyk, James Gaskin, Judi Fleming, Marilyn Breithart, Annabel Smyth, Terence Wright, Alexander von Thorn, M. Barnard, Erin Barrett-Hamner, Stanley Shursky, Kimberly Borrowdale, Bill Quick and Loren MacGregor for attempting (but not, I hope, succeeding) to give me a big head, and for all those wild and wonderful ideas and suggestions.

« Prologue »

Richard Lennox held life in his hands. He cradled it carefully as he strode towards the airlock at the far end of the environmentally controlled section of his laboratory.

Around him, rows of shallow culture tanks spread out under the harsh glare of the spectrum-modified halide strip-lamps. The light bounced off the acres of white tile and brushed steel of the room, and turned the algae growing in the tanks emerald green.

Green – the colour of Phodex, his wonderful high-protein algae. Green – the colour of money.

Richard Lennox was going to feed the world. Just as long as the world could afford to pay.

He would have smiled, but for the mask that covered his mouth and nose. He sucked in air and glanced up at the LED above the airlock. Six, it said. That was the percentage of oxygen in the room's atmosphere. Reflexively, he looked down at the read-out on the little compressed air cylinder that swung from his shoulder: there was a good twenty minutes left in it – he'd known he still had plenty of air left, but he'd never outgrown the habit of checking at regular intervals.

He stopped at one of the tanks. The surface was covered with thick green sludge, like a stagnant pond. As he watched, a gas bubble rose to the surface, hung there for a moment, and then popped. He held the stoppered and sealed jar containing the Phodex seed material up to the light. Spores in brown clumps as large as his little fingernail hung suspended in nutrient solution. If the whole contents of this room were destroyed, there was enough material here to start again from scratch.

But that would take time, and Lennox had given the Phodex project years of his life already. He didn't intend to let it happen.

He transferred the jar to his left hand, and stirred the nutrient liquid in which the algae was growing with his fingers. He'd found during his experiments that its consistency was as good a guide to the health of the plants as any of his carefully controlled experiments. This was just right – slightly viscid and almost greasy. Phodex was derived from a freshwater algae, but there were substances in the nutrient solution that speeded up its growth. Those, of course, were his secret.

'Good,' he murmured as he reached the airlock. The red light that flooded the inner chamber glowed eerily through the reinforced glass of the window. He grunted as he pushed the heavy steel handle. It swung slowly round, and the door opened. He stepped through. The chamber was small – barely big enough for three people. He let the inner door thud shut. Almost immediately, a red light winked above his head, showing the seal was good. Only then did he push open the outer door.

Peter Glass, New Earth Foods' head of security, was waiting for him in the monitoring room. The man was dressed in a dark suit, smart enough to pass in any company, but not so sharp as to arouse comment.

Lennox handed over the jar. Glass took it gingerly.

Lennox pulled his mask down, muttering, 'Thank you, Mr Glass,' as he did so. He turned to hang up the mask next to the others on the rack. The door and walls were covered in warning signs. Lennox ignored them – he'd seen them a hundred, a thousand times.

He strode away, letting Glass follow him through the monitoring room.

'I think this is a little excessive, Mr Lennox, if I may say so,' Glass said. He shut the door behind them. 'Our present security is perfectly adequate, sir.' The lights flickered off as they left the room and came on ahead of them automatically as they walked down the corridor.

Lennox scowled. It seemed he had a security chief more concerned with energy conservation than ensuring the safety of his charges.

Around them, the labs and offices of New Earth Foods were spread out around a central concourse of pierced metal sheeting and pipes enamelled in bright blue, white and yellow – New Earth Foods' corporate colours. This late, the whole place was deserted. Only the hum of the air-conditioning broke the silence.

He ran up the stairs that led to his private offices. 'Maybe, Glass,' he said. He was only a little out of breath. 'But if all goes well, Phodex will make this company very rich.'

He went through into his office. Through the sheet-glass walls, he could see the city spread out below them: chains and clusters of lights picking out the roads and homes and all the structures of human habitation in gold and ruby and emerald.

All those people, he thought: soon they'll know my name.

A nondescript black saloon purred quietly into the car-park of New Earth Foods, where the actinic light of

3

half a hundred street lamps sent grotesque shadows jagging across the empty expanse of tarmac.

The saloon stopped in the dark shelter of the sprawling glass and metal building, and two men got out. Both were dressed in red jumpsuits and full-face masks. Ambrose, the first man out, passed a torch and holdall to his companion, Wilson.

He glanced up. A single office was lit, several storeys above the ground, and he could see two people moving around inside like characters on some giant television screen in the sky. He nodded to Wilson, and they set off at a trot towards the building. They ran past the front entrance and headed towards the service area at the back.

Ambrose arrived at the service door first. He grasped the knob and twisted it. The cold of the brushed aluminium bit through the thin leather of his gloves. For a second, the knob wouldn't move.

He frowned, wondering if this was the wrong door. But through the glass he could clearly see the monitoring room. It was shadowed, illuminated only by the overspill from the car-park lighting and the dull glare of row upon row of computer monitors. On the far side, a door was clearly marked 'Propagation Suite'.

Come on, he thought at the knob, come *on*. The door was supposed to be open. If it wasn't, they'd have to find another way in. The whole operation would be in jeopardy. So would the money he'd been promised for doing it.

Then the knob twisted. He eased the door open and slid inside the room. Wilson followed him, then darted ahead to the Propagation Suite door. He punched in the combination they'd been given, and then the maintenance override that stopped the airlock going through the cycle that ensured no oxygen-rich air got into the Propagation Room.

4

Ambrose watched the door that led to the rest of the building. Any minute now, the lights will go on. Sirens will wail – no, the door had a silent alarm on it. That's it: we've been set up –

A movement of air brushed his back with cool fingers. He turned. Wilson had opened the Propagation Suite door. As Ambrose hurried over, Wilson grabbed a breathing mask from the rack on the wall. Ambrose did the same. He fitted the mask snugly over his nose and mouth. The cylinder was very light – can't contain more than a few minutes of compressed air, he thought. But that would be enough.

Wilson pushed open the inner door. Harsh light flooded out. Beyond the door, rows of tanks spread out in all directions.

Ambrose hurried across to a tank close by. It was filled with liquid and a lurid green plant that reminded him of seaweed. He pulled a jar out of his holdall and began to fill it with the plant.

Bleep.

He looked round to identify the source of the sound, but couldn't.

Bleep.

Just as long as it isn't an alarm, he thought. He glanced at Wilson, who shrugged and continued to fill his jar.

Bleep. Bleep.

This time, Ambrose took a longer look round. Finally, he saw a red LED above the door. It showed a figure – 10.

Bleepbleepbleep.

The figure changed with each sound – 11, 12, 13.

Ambrose didn't like the look of that. Hurriedly, he scooped another handful of the plant into his jar.

Another forty seconds, he thought – just another forty seconds and they'd be away.

Bleepbleepbleep.

Lennox gestured at the safe he'd had specially installed. It was a shining titanium sphere which picked up the neon lights that slanted through the wall-length office windows.

'As you can see, Mr Glass, I'm not taking any chances,' he said. He slid open the door.

Glass watched him impassively, his face turned ghostly by the blue-white light shining from inside the safe. 'I'm glad to see that, Mr Lennox,' he said.

'This new safe is controlled by a computerised time-lock – once-a-week access only,' Lennox said as he took the jar of Phodex seed material from the security chief and placed it gently in the safe. 'That will keep the seed material secure while Phodex gets its public launch.' Glass nodded. Lennox waited for him to go away – surely the man realised that the fewer people who knew the password, the safer the Phodex would be? But Glass just stood there nodding his head as if he understood everything. 'I'm going to enter the password now,' Lennox said. Still Glass stayed where he was, nodding wisely. 'If you don't mind, Mr Glass, best I keep this to myself,' Lennox said, finally unable to keep the impatience out of his voice.

Reluctantly, Glass turned away. He went and stood over by the window. Lennox pushed the safe door, and it thudded softly shut. The display flashed a request for him to input his chosen password. He did so, and clicked the enter button. The green telltale on the door winked on, indicating that the timelock had engaged.

That's it, Lennox thought. No matter what happens, the Phodex is safe now.

The monitor speakers began to whoop.

* * *

6

Lennox thundered down the stairs two at a time, but fast as he was, Glass was faster. The security chief got to the bottom, pounded across the office and shouldered open the door to the monitoring room.

Lennox heard him shout: 'What the hell do you think you're up to?'

Glass grunted and there was a dull thud.

Lennox got to the door. He took in the scene at a glance – Glass on the floor, the Propagation Suite door standing open, the monitors all displaying *Warning Oxygen Level High*. And the two masked men running towards the outer door. Lennox pelted after them, but they were too fast.

By the time he reached the door, they were leaping into a car that had obviously been waiting for them. Lennox slapped the alarm, and the sirens began to wail.

Ambrose gunned the car. It started first time and he floored the accelerator. The car screamed away from the building, the squeal of its tyres momentarily drowning out the howl of the alarms.

It was a crying shame the monitors had gone off – up till then it had been easy. Well, for what they were paying him he hadn't expected it to be easy.

Their headlights raked the tarmac. They still had time enough to get away. He swung the saloon round and headed for the car-park exit.

'Damn!' he swore as he saw the heavy metal bar coming down in front of him. He pumped the accelerator, but the engine had nothing left to give. 'Brace!' he yelled as he went for it.

The car whacked into the barrier. Ambrose was slammed back into his seat and for a second he lost control of the wheel. Beside him, Wilson grunted.

The windscreen shattered into a million pieces. It

7

stayed in its frame, though, making it impossible to see out.

Outside the car, Ambrose could hear the chugging of a powerful diesel engine. Traffic. At this time of night.

Hell.

'Get rid of it!' he screamed.

Wilson jack-knifed in his seat and kicked the glass away. Cold air battered Ambrose like a fist.

An articulated lorry filled his vision like a white wall. He yanked the steering wheel. But it was too late.

The bonnet of the car slid under the lorry. There was a split second when Ambrose knew what was going to happen. He got his arms up in front of his face. Tasted coppery fear as the white wall expanded to become everything in the universe.

He heard screaming and realised, distantly, that it was himself. Then he hit the wall, and for a moment there was an infinity of pain and heat.

And then, as from a very great distance, the sound of sirens.

« One »

Ros was on her third cup of coffee of the morning when Ed walked in with the parcel. 'What's this? Someone's birthday?' she asked.

'Courier delivery,' Ed said. 'Addressed personally to you, Ros.' He put the parcel down on the floor.

Beckett swung round in his chair. 'You checked it out?' he asked. He scowled suspiciously at the parcel, which was wrapped in zebra-stripe paper.

'Relax,' Ed said. 'I ran it through the ultra-sonic scanner. It's as sound as –'

'Don't say it,' Ros said. She put her cup down and went over to the parcel. There was a Stross Cybertech hologram sticker on the side. 'Oh,' she said. 'It's from Charlie.'

She popped the tab on the box and the lid sprang open. Inside, there was a gadget nestling within shock-absorbing gel pads. She pulled it out. The thing was the size of a large key-ring, and had a tiny parabolic emitter on the front, plus a few buttons and a read-out on the back. Ros scowled at it. She had a very simple attitude to gadgets: she ought to be able to understand how they worked just by looking at

9

them; but this was just a mystery to her.

Ed fished around in the box for a second.

'I am *not* reading the instructions, Ed,' she said.

But all he handed her was a small plastic card bearing the Stross Cybertech logo. She grinned at it ruefully and pressed the activation pad in the corner. Immediately the logo swirled and reformed into a moving image of Charlie, a chubby man in his early thirties, with a fuzz of black hair and beard so wild they formed an almost perfect circle round his head.

'Hi Ros,' Charlie's picture said. 'As promised, here's the prototype of the SID I said I'd send you.'

'SID?' Beckett asked.

'Sonic Infiltration Device,' Ros said.

Ed pulled a face that said he'd believe it when he saw it – whatever it was.

Charlie went on: 'Think of it as a sonic screwdriver, and you won't go far wrong. I'm giving a paper on it, and some of our other new audio-based goodies, like sound-suppression equipment and non-lethal sonic-based weaponry, at the seminar on Expert Systems for Security Management in a couple of days – shame you can't be there.' A peculiar glint came into Charlie's eyes. 'Anyway, about the SID – it's perfectly simple to use, but we've managed to cram in five gigs of compressed probe-and-predict software, piggybacked to a phased sonic –'

Hurriedly, Ros pressed the activation pad again. Charlie grinned at her for a second, and then the picture swirled and re-formed into the Stross Cybertech logo. 'That's quite enough of that, Charlie,' she said.

Ed frowned. 'Sonic Infiltration Device?' he asked.

'He only mentioned it in passing,' Ros muttered. 'I never thought he'd send one – probably thinks he's going to get it field-tested on the cheap.' She stared at the SID for a second. 'Only one way to find out,' she said. She pressed the button that most looked like an activator.

'I wouldn't do that,' Ed said.

There was a squeal so high-pitched it was barely audible.

'I really wouldn't do that,' Beckett added.

All the alarms in the Gizmos building went off at the same time.

'Nice one, Charlie,' Ros said, and smiled.

Biology wasn't Ros's speciality. She preferred gadgets – they did what they were told and you didn't have to feed them.

But she did think she knew a thing or two about marketing, especially since she'd kept Gizmos going when the previous owner had sold up.

Bearing that in mind, she reckoned Richard Lennox was a man with a bigger problem than mere security. Security she could take care of, with a little help from her friends. Persuading the public at large that they wanted to eat a slimy green plant for breakfast, lunch and supper might be beyond even her.

So it was just as well that wasn't her problem.

She leant back against the leather seats in the boardroom of New Earth Foods. Beckett and Ed were either side of her, and they were all waiting for Lennox to arrive. She could see that Ed was already getting impatient – to him, sitting around waiting to be briefed was a far worse part of any assignment than scaling the sheer side of a three-hundred-foot tower block, or flying a copter with one rotor out and only ten minutes of fuel left. He drummed impatiently on the soft leather with his fingers.

As for Beckett, he stared impassively out of the window. If she hadn't known him better, Ros would have assumed he was bored and thinking about anything other than New Earth Foods and its security problems. But Ros knew he had been working from the moment they first entered the building. By now he would have built up a mental blueprint of the entire building: entrances, exits, video monitoring and – perhaps more importantly – blindspots. She wondered what he'd made of Lennox. To her, he'd seemed like an untidy heap of a man, all crumpled white coat and scraggly grey hair; and a flutterer with it, though she had to admit he must be quite bright to have developed Phodex and built up New Earth Foods. Beckett though, would have seen through the fluster and bluster – he'd know whether they were dealing with a genius who could only handle so much real life, or one who had carefully developed that image to put people off-guard.

As she mused, Lennox came in. He put a plate of canapés down on the smoked glass coffee table in front of them. Then he sat down next to Beckett and pointed his remote control at the television on the far side of the room. It flickered into life and a catchy tune started up as the New Earth Foods corporate logo appeared on the screen. That faded, and a picture of a rushing river took its place.

'The story of Phodex starts in Brazil, where in the upper reaches of the Amazon is found the native algae called Phytex Monginus,' said the narrator in well-rounded actorly tones.

Ros leant forward and helped herself to a snack – a tiny sliver of smoked salmon on a cracker. It was some of the best she'd ever tasted. Whatever else she might think about Lennox, he certainly knew how to treat his guests. She looked back at the screen.

The Amazon had been replaced by a close-up of a piece of the weed. Algae, she corrected herself as the narrator continued: 'This algae is a natural source of many vitamins and trace elements.'

It was large-leaved and a deep spinach green. Ros had never liked spinach. Besides, it looked a bit slimy. She grinned and glanced at Ed. He looked slightly ill. Beckett was wearing his usual believe-it-when-I-see-it expression. As for herself – well, she had a deep-rooted belief that science could do just about anything – if the scientists had the drive and the intelligence to ask the right questions. She leant forward and helped herself to another canapé – cheese this time, strong enough to make her mouth sting, and with a pleasantly nutty aftertaste.

'Doesn't look exactly consumer-friendly, does it?' she asked no one in particular.

'This new variety has been genetically engineered to produce an entirely new strain with increased nutritional value . . .' the narrator went on.

Beckett seemed about as interested in the presentation as Ros was – which was to say, to the exact extent that it would help them carry out the assignment Lennox had given them, but no more than that. He reached over and took a canapé without taking his eyes from the screen.

A smile played across Lennox's lips. Ros frowned, but now the narrator was explaining that Phodex was going to become the food of the future. A series of stills flashed across the screen – potatoes, rice, mushrooms, cod fillet. 'Phodex is the food of the future,' the narrator finished portentously.

'Dream on!' Ed muttered. Good old Ed, Ros thought – never mind that Lennox was in the room with them, he could be relied on to say what they were all thinking. 'You can't possibly make all that food out of that . . . that . . . weed!'

Lennox didn't seem to mind the outburst in the least.

He turned the television off, then got up and strolled over to the coffee table, from where he could see them all at once.

'How were the canapés?' he asked, as if it followed naturally from what Ed had said.

'Good,' Beckett said shortly. He glared at the television screen, clearly wishing Lennox would hurry up and brief them.

'Great,' Ros added. 'Thanks.' She took one of the few remaining cheese ones. They were far too good to let them go to waste.

'Phodex,' Lennox said.

No one said anything. For a second Ros assumed Lennox was going to continue where the video had left off, and tell them a great deal of irrelevant detail about genetic engineering and which genes they'd spliced in to which sections of the Phytex DNA. He didn't. He just stood there grinning like a magician who had just completed a particularly difficult trick.

'I'm sorry?' Beckett asked eventually.

'It's all made out of Phodex,' Lennox said patiently.

Ros paused with the canapé halfway to her mouth.

'Smoked salmon,' Beckett said.

'Cheddar cheese.' Ros stared suspiciously at the canapé.

Ed reached out and picked one of them up as gingerly as if it was so much high explosive primed to go off.

'Phodex,' Lennox said firmly.

Ed put the canapé back down on the tray.

Beckett followed Lennox out of the boardroom and into the main concourse of New Earth Foods. Ed and Ros were just behind, content for now to let him take the lead.

He thought he had Lennox's measure now. He'd met

the type before: content to let the world think he was an amiable buffoon, just as long as it furthered his plans. His little presentation had been well thought-out and neatly timed, though. It had convinced the Gizmos team of Phodex's potential far faster than any sales pitch could have.

No, Lennox was far from a buffoon – and that meant his enemies, whoever they were, were far from that too. Otherwise he would long since have dealt with them.

Lennox led the way to an open-plan staircase made of pierced metal and white pipe. 'It looks like common-or-garden pondweed,' he said as they climbed the steps. He sounded slightly breathless, but the pace he set was a good one. He turned back to face Beckett. 'But it's far from common and you won't find it in your garden.'

They reached the top of the stairs. A young woman, dressed like Lennox in a white lab coat, was waiting for them. She was thin and pale-skinned, with a shock of short dark hair. Pretty in a sharp-featured sort of way, Beckett thought, and realised she was staring at him. Yes, he decided – definitely pretty.

'Now,' Lennox said, 'this is Sally, my research assistant.'

She was standing in front of a table on which was a large tank. It was half filled with scummy green water, and there were white strip lights attached to its steel cover.

'Right, Sally – do the honours please,' Lennox said when they had gathered round the table.

Sally lifted the lid off the tank and put it to one side.

Ed frowned. 'Now, the guys who broke in were after this?' he asked. He sounded disbelieving.

'The food industry's desperate to develop something like this,' Sally said. Her voice was surprisingly deep, with just a trace of an accent Beckett couldn't quite place. Not that it was relevant to the job in hand, he told himself firmly. She picked up a strainer and fished out a spoonful of the algae.

'It's the Holy Grail,' Lennox pronounced. 'Food for the next millennium.'

Beckett wondered how long it had taken his marketing agency to come up with that one, and how much they'd charged him.

He thrust his hands deeper into the pockets of his leather jacket. It was time to get down to business. 'So,' he said, 'straightforward industrial espionage.'

He glanced at Ros and Ed. This was a staple of what they did, something they all understood. Now they'd answered the 'What', the only question remaining was 'Who'. After that it would be business as usual.

'Zander,' Lennox said. 'He's been trying to put me out of business for years.' He stared at them expectantly, as if they ought to know who he was talking about.

'Zander?' Ros asked.

Sally reached for a disposable wipe and started to dry the strainer. 'He's their Research Director,' she said, and smiled straight at Beckett. He stared at her blankly. Like most of the specialists he'd ever met, Lennox and Sally obviously couldn't believe that the important people in their own little world were unknown outside it. 'He runs Hennessey-Brock,' she went on, as if that explained everything.

Lennox chewed his bottom lip. 'They're the sharks of the food industry,' he said. 'They want to swallow my company.' Suddenly he sounded like a sulky little boy who'd been threatened with having his toys taken away. 'They'll do anything to get their hands on this.'

Beckett stared at the murky green mess in the tank. From what Lennox had said, it had the potential to make billions for its owner.

16

He glanced from it to Sally. She was smiling at him. He found himself beginning to smile back, and forced his face back into its habitual scowl.

Business was business. And it came first, last, and always.

« Two »

Beckett parked his jeep across the street from the canopied entrance of the Hennessey-Brock offices. He glanced at Ed, then shaded his eyes against the sun and stared up, and up, and up. The vast blue-glass tower of the building speared the sky. Big money. If he knew anything about such places – and he knew a lot about them – the chief executive officer's office was to be found on the top floor, on the outer edge; perhaps on a corner. The more important the executive, the more windows they were entitled to.

Besides, he'd discovered one thing during his time first at the Hive and then working with Ros: if he encountered a tall building during a job, he was sure to have to go right to the top of it at some stage.

He felt dizzy just thinking about it.

'Penthouse suite?' Ed asked, mirroring his thoughts.

Beckett nodded, thoughtfully. He was already considering how to get inside. They could try a straight-forward break in, but that would mean waiting till dark, and however much Ed might enjoy scaling the sides of that man-made mountain of glass, they couldn't spare the time. Ros had been playing with lasers which, focused on the windows of a room, could transmit anything said by the people inside; but that meant finding out which room they needed, and then a building that overlooked it, and the offices surrounding Hennessey-Brock were low-built.

'The air-conditioning?' Ed asked. 'That's worked before.'

Anything so he could get his adrenalin rush by sneaking around one step ahead of Hennessey-Brock's security staff, Beckett thought. 'Too obvious,' he said firmly.

'What do you want to go for then?' Ed asked.

'The jugular,' Beckett said, and smiled wolfishly.

Ed pulled his workman's hard-hat down over his eyes in what he hoped was a businesslike fashion. He resisted the urge to check the street either side of the Hennessey-Brock building for observers, then squatted in front of the casing of the Primary Connection Interface for the company's telecommunications.

I'm doing my job, he thought. Just an everyday CommEx maintenance man, checking a few connections here and there . . . He wiped the electronic jemmy Ros had given him through the slot, and the casing slid up with the faintest whirr of its servo-motor. Here we go, Ed thought, surveying the racks of IC boards.

'I'll have to be quick, it's a forty-line exchange,' he sub-vocalised into the microphone hidden beneath a synthetic skin patch on his mastoid bone. He hated the thing – it itched terribly, and he was sure he'd get a rash from it – but, as Ros had pointed out, it was a lot less noticeable than the mike-set he usually wore, and that was important when he was working out in the open like this.

'You always are, aren't you?' Beckett said.

Ed didn't bother to reply. He was too busy attaching

the leads of the frequency scanner to the boards in the Interface Cabinet. He took a deep breath. 'And here's one I prepared earlier,' he muttered to himself.

'What's that?' Beckett demanded.

'That's a go,' Ed said, realising what he'd done. That was the other reason he hated the bone-mike – you had to watch every word you said.

He glanced over at the car. Beckett leant out of the window and pointed the device Charlie had sent them at the Alarm Control Centre on the side of the Hennessey-Brock building.

'Do your stuff, you little beauty,' Ed thought, and only realised he'd spoken aloud when Beckett asked if he had a problem.

A second later, all hell let loose. First the exterior intruder alarms started up, with a hideous two-tone yowl. Next, the fire alarms added a counterpoint in perfect disharmony. Inside the foyer, the fire sprinklers came on, and the overhead lights were diffracted into a thousand tiny rainbows by the water droplets.

The lights on Ed's board started to flash red as phones all over the building began to be used. Here we go, he thought, remembering not to sub-vocalise. A green light winked on next to the LCD display, which changed to read 'Match Found'. Ed flipped a switch, diverting the call from its intended recipient to himself.

'Hello?' a man's voice shouted over the wailing of alarms. 'Is that JBS Security?'

'Hello, JBS Security, how may I help you?' Ed said in his best man-in-a-suit voice.

'This is Harris here, at Hennessey-Brock,' yelled the man. 'It's our alarm system – it's gone crazy.'

'I see,' Ed said.

'How soon can you get someone out here?' Harris asked.

'We'll have someone with you right away, sir,' Ed said. Better make it convincing. He asked for Harris's details, and pretended to write them down. Then he broke the connection.

He dismantled his equipment, and closed up the Primary Interface Cabinet. Then he dogtrotted towards Beckett's jeep.

After all, he had promised Mr Harris they'd be there soon.

The young man behind the registration desk at the Expert Systems for Security Management Seminar smiled. He was paid to smile.

The man he was smiling at scowled back at him.

Beckett strode into the Hennessey-Brock building, ignoring the water cascading from the overhead sprinklers. The receptionist was less accepting of it. She scowled at them as her expensive hairdo plastered itself in little ringlets around her immaculately made-up face.

'Yes?' she demanded as Ed and Beckett approached.

Beckett pulled out his JBS security pass. Ed did the same. 'We're here to see a Mr Harris,' Beckett said.

The receptionist pulled a face. 'I've not seen these before –'

Blast, Beckett thought. He'd faked the passes up in the car – printed them out in full colour and laminated them, complete with false ID numbers – but he'd had to make an inspired guess at the JBS logo. Apparently it wasn't inspired enough.

'New logo,' Ed said. 'Corporate redesign – apparently our lords and masters think they're making too much money, so they've decided to spend some of it on new company stationery.'

The receptionist thought about that for a second. Ed smiled at her. It had the desired effect. Then again, it usually did. Clever little so and so, Beckett thought admiringly as they walked across to the Security Control Room.

Ed lounged against the brushed chrome wall, where he could see anyone who might be coming their way without seeming to be keeping guard; while Beckett pressed his electronic pick against the cupboard lock. He raised an eyebrow at Ed. It wouldn't do to be seen using something other than the correct JBS-issued key to open the cupboard. Ed nodded almost imperceptibly, and Beckett activated the pick. Twin prongs slid out and into the lock. The pick added its own high-pitched whine to the cacophony; but only for an instant. Then the door sprang open. Beckett reset the system, and the alarms died away.

'Good,' he said.

'Better than that,' Ed said. He gestured to a board on the wall opposite the control room. 'Research and Development, floor fifty-three.'

Beckett scowled at the board, wishing what it said would change just to please him. It didn't. 'Floor fifty-three it is,' he said.

Ros slid her scanner along the channel in the doorframe that held the security wiring. The hand-held device beeped regularly as she moved it. Glass peered over her shoulder. She wondered if he understood what the flickering lights on the display meant. She rather thought not – partly because she'd made the scanner for the use of the team and had never bothered prettying it up for the general public; and partly because as far as she could tell, as a Chief of Security, Peter Glass was about as much use as an old-style valve in a modern computer.

Still, New Earth Foods was employing them, so she supposed she'd have to humour him. 'See,' she said, pointing at the unbroken line of wiring. 'The sensor reeds here are completely untouched.'

'But this was the door the intruders used,' Glass said. He sounded genuinely bewildered.

'And there's no sign of any bypass,' Ros said. She walked round the door, checking the inside of the glass with her fingers just to be sure. Besides, she was rather hoping Glass might redeem himself. If he'd worked it out, he didn't let on, but just stood gawping past Ros at the interior of the Propagation Suite, where a group of technicians were bustling around, getting ready to leave for the evening. 'I'd say someone left it open for them,' Ros said at last.

'Oh I don't think so,' Glass said. 'Our security arrangements are very tight – really very tight indeed –'

That's what they all say, Ros thought, but she didn't say it. 'I think I'd better have a look at your personnel files,' she said.

'Well, if you must,' Glass answered. 'But I really ought to get authorisation from Mr –'

'I must,' Ros said, starting through the outer area of the Propagation Complex towards the nearest computer console. 'And Mr Lennox already authorised us to do whatever we needed, remember?' She repressed a sigh. It was always the way. Glass had messed up royally by allowing the raiders to gain access; he was just bright enough to know he wasn't very bright, and now he was determined not to mess up again – and that meant he was paranoid about everything, including Ros, Ed and Beckett.

If there was one thing that guaranteed that this job was going to be trouble, it was probably Peter Glass getting under their feet.

Well, they'd dealt with far worse and survived, she thought as she dumped her holdall by the console and seated herself at the computer. And after all, how dangerous could a tank of pondweed be – even if it were a tank of artificially mutated, genetically enhanced pondweed?

She opened the personnel record file, but waited for Glass to use his password to let her log on: she could as well have managed without, but it probably wouldn't do any harm to humour him for a while. It wasn't as if he didn't want to help – he was just completely ineffectual.

'Here we go,' Glass said as a screenful of names flashed up. 'Current personnel roster.' He said it with the air of a magician producing a particularly fat and glossy white rabbit from a hat. Perhaps he thought he'd impressed her. 'Our security passes log us in and out,' Glass explained. 'You can easily find out who was here last night.'

Ros didn't bother to tell him she'd known that as soon as she'd looked at the sensors on the door. She stared at the screen for a moment, wondering if Glass would get all excited if she loaded up a little search program of her own to speed things up. New Earth Foods had a lot of employees, and if she had to check every file manually, she'd still be looking at sunrise.

Before she could make her mind up, Glass said, 'Oh!' Ros twisted round. 'This staff list needs updating,' he said. Surprise me, Ros thought; Peter Glass's security system had more holes in it than a fishing net. 'James Fricker died months ago, poor man. Something to do with Phodex.' He said the word as if it were unfamiliar to him – he probably didn't think the company's business was anything to do with him. He was wrong, in Ros's opinion. You couldn't keep anything secure unless you kept one step ahead of the opposition, and you couldn't do that unless you knew what they were likely to go after – and that, in turn, meant knowing what your client was about.

'Don't mention it to Mr Lennox.' Glass's voice interrupted Ros's train of thought. 'He doesn't like to talk about it –'

Does he not? Ros wondered. She turned round to look at Glass. He seemed genuinely worried. 'Really?' she said. Something else Glass had obviously never worked out: you couldn't protect someone if you were scared even to talk to them.

She clicked on James Fricker's file.

'Oh I wouldn't do that –' Glass said.

He needn't have worried. The words 'Confidential – Access Denied' flashed up on the screen in bright red letters an inch high.

We'll see about that, Ros thought; but first she wanted to have a word with Lennox. Besides, she'd have to get rid of Glass. The poor man would probably develop apoplexy when he realised what she was going to do to his precious file system.

The world dropped away beneath Beckett as the cylindrical glass elevator hurtled up the side of the Hennessey-Brock building. The acceleration bore down on him, pinning him to the transparent floor of the elevator. He felt his hands go sweaty even though his rational mind knew there were two layers of polycarbon-reinforced glass between him and the open air.

He forced himself to look straight ahead. Better. He counted the storeys of the lower surrounding buildings as they passed them. Ten. Twelve. Fifteen. At, say, four metres a storey, that was sixty metres.

Make that sixty-four. They'd just passed another layer of windows.

He glanced down. That was a mistake. His jeep looked like a toy car, and even as he watched it got smaller.

'Must be nearly a third of the way there,' Ed said cheerfully.

Beckett smiled thinly.

The elevator took them up past the roofs of the surrounding buildings.

Beckett wondered whether there was any chance they'd hit the cloud layer.

Lennox leant back and let the massage unit in his chair begin to knead his neck and shoulders. He clicked on his word processor and spoke into the microphone: 'Press Release – For Immediate Action.' The words appeared on the screen in front of him. 'On Tuesday the world will see –'

His office door opened. Ros walked in and planted herself in front of his desk. He swung round to face her. 'What can I do for you?' He'd really hoped her team would deal with Hennessey-Brock and leave him to get on with more important things, such as setting up the Phodex launch – but he supposed if she needed help, he'd better be prepared to give it.

'Tell me about James Fricker,' she said.

'Fricker?' he said, startled. He'd almost managed to put that unpleasant business out of his mind. After all, in any pioneering venture, a few hardy souls were likely to prove – well – not hardy enough. As had James Fricker. 'Fricker's death...' He paused, considering how best to close down what could only be a fruitless line of enquiry. He steepled his hands in front of him, knowing it gave him a statesmanlike air. 'Fricker's death is an internal company matter.' He saw her gathering a protest. 'And outside your brief,' he said firmly.

'Is the process of making Phodex dangerous at all?' she demanded.

She was obviously bright, Lennox thought: perhaps too bright. Worse, she had no understanding of the practicalities. 'Of course not,' he said, glad he was able to answer honestly. 'Unless you're stupid enough to fall into the tanks or forget to wear your oxygen mask –'

'And Mr Fricker?' Ros asked. 'Was he stupid enough to fall into a tank of Phodex?'

'No,' Lennox said, suddenly bored with the whole conversation. 'And before you ask, he didn't forget his oxygen mask, either. Now forget him.' He glared at her. She looked back at him levelly, and he suddenly realised that if it came to a staring competition, he'd lose every time. 'Just find out which of my staff is a traitor.'

She raised her eyebrows. It took Lennox a moment to realise she was surprised that Glass had already told him her earlier findings, about the outer door being left open.

'Now,' he said, 'if there's nothing else, I'm very busy –'

'That'll be all – for now,' she said. She turned and left, her sensible flat shoes making no sound at all on the deep-pile carpet.

Lennox swung back to his word processor, wondering why that sounded quite so much like a threat. He stared gloomily at the screen for a second before he realised that the processor had faithfully transcribed every word of the conversation.

'Delete document,' he said wearily, and prepared to begin again.

« Three »

Doctor Charles Stross clicked off his laser pointer. The screen showing his data faded, and the house lights went up. He thanked the audience for listening to him. Meanwhile his assistants packed away his equipment.

Of most interest to Rafael D'Angelo was a small device consisting of a parabolic shield emitter on top of a box of electronic wizardry.

From the demonstration Stross had just given, it could do everything D'Angelo's contacts had said it could.

He stood up and pushed his way out of the auditorium. He had seen enough. More than enough.

He smiled to himself as he moved through the herd of scientists. Who needed to be able to invent such clever devices, he thought, when the strong could simply take what they required?

The door to Zander's office was no match for Beckett's electronic pick. He pulled the tiny device out of the lock and pocketed it, then eased the door open.

He'd been right about one thing – Zander rated two floor-to-ceiling windows. The city lay spread out before them under a sky the colour of pearl.

Nice if you liked that kind of thing, Beckett thought.

He ignored it and led the way into the room, with Ed close behind.

'You take that,' he said, nodding to the half-acre or so of chromed steel and smoked glass that Zander used as a desk.

Ed nodded, and went straight over to it. Meanwhile Beckett flipped up a small access hatch in the floor, underneath which there were a couple of spare power sockets and the routing boxes for Zander's phone and computer.

'Want me to copy his hard disk?' Ed asked.

'No time,' Beckett said. 'Anyway, we can pull out anything we want by remote.'

He took a phone bug out of an anti-static pouch in his case. Ten seconds later he'd fitted it between the routing box and Zander's phone, and was confident Zander would never know the difference.

Now for the computer, he thought. Of course, they could just hack in, but that would be a lot more work and –

'Look at this,' Ed said. Beckett glanced up. Ed was holding out a New Earth Foods folder. ' "An announcement of Phodex from New Earth Foods",' he read.

'No harm having a press release, Ed,' Beckett said. Ed was a good man to have at your back, but he did get a bit excited about things at times.

'Nor in having a keen interest in photography,' Ed agreed, ignoring Beckett's sarcasm as he usually did. 'But check this out.'

This time he came round the desk to where Beckett was working. He crouched down and handed a sheaf of eight-by-ten photographs to Beckett.

Beckett stared at them. The green glass dome of the

restaurant, with its plant-festooned interior, was un-mistakable. A discreet sign proclaimed it to be The Green Machine restaurant. 'Hey wait a minute –' he said.

'It's where they're having the Phodex launch,' Ed confirmed. 'What are these guys planning?'

Beckett shrugged. That, after all, was what they were being paid to discover.

The phone rang.

Beckett stared at it. He'd known it was all too easy, and that their luck would run out sometime. It seemed that time had come.

Someone would come to answer the phone.

Beckett flipped the access cover shut. The phone bug was in place, but not the one on the computer. He stared wildly round the room, looking for a place to hide or, better yet, a means of escape.

Nothing. Nothing but a two hundred metre freefall through the chilly air.

The phone shrilled on.

There had to be something. There was always something.

Ed grabbed his sleeve. He turned, and looked at where Ed was pointing. Sanctuary. A door in the wall – a way out? A built-in cupboard?

Beckett didn't care and didn't have time to worry.

Ed opened the door. It led into a cupboard – there were a few packets of paper on the shelves – barely big enough for one of them, never mind two. Nevertheless, they crammed themselves into it. Ed got the door shut just as they heard the sound of the outer door opening. He held it closed with one hand, which meant he had to reach across Beckett, who got a mouthful of leather jacket to go with Ed's knee which was grinding into the small of his back.

He squatted in the darkness, scarcely daring to breathe.

31

A muscle in his calf started to jump. It's only pain, he thought. Ignore it.

Footsteps – very quiet on the carpet. The sound of the phone being picked up. The ringing stopped.

Then: 'Zander –' very businesslike. Paydirt! Beckett thought. But then Zander's tone softened. 'Hi,' he said. Beckett could imagine the relaxed, open posture, the smile that would somehow translate itself to the listener. Zander was talking to a woman – a girlfriend, Beckett was sure.

Ed nudged Beckett, who looked up at him. With his free hand, Ed cupped his ear.

Of course, Beckett thought – the bug. He slipped the receiver into his ear.

'Hi yourself,' said a voice. It was flat, almost genderless, though Beckett thought it was almost certainly female; to his experienced ear it was obvious that it had been distorted by an audio-modification unit. He didn't recognise it, but that hardly mattered – the fact that the voice was disguised meant the owner had to be Zander's mole. With a bit of luck they'd go on to discuss their new plans.

'I'm sorry about last night.'

Apparently that didn't impress Zander. 'I can't risk another disaster like that,' he said. There was nothing gentle in his voice – rather, his tones were clipped, almost military. 'You'll just have to try harder.'

'But it's so difficult,' the voice said. 'Lennox has got this place cinched down so tight –'

'That's why I need you there – on the inside –'

'Yes, I know. But now he's brought in this team of security experts . . . there are surveillance guys crawling all over the place and –'

'Surveillance guys?' Zander cut in. He paused. Beckett could just imagine him, looking around, suddenly worried he was being spied on. There's none so

32

paranoid as those engaged in the illicit. He was right of course, but that wasn't the point. 'Who are they?'

'Well, I don't know,' the voice said impatiently. 'Lennox hired them, not me!'

Zander didn't reply. Straining to hear what was going on, Beckett made out the sound of soft footfalls, then creaking leather. Dammit, he thought – Zander's settling in for a long session. He glanced at Ed. They might get some useful information – though nothing they couldn't get from the comfort of the jeep – but the longer they stayed the greater the chance they'd be discovered, especially since he'd developed a cramp in his left calf.

Zander and the mole continued to talk, though they said nothing that gave away their future plans.

The only strategy he could think of was high-risk. But that was okay. High-risk meant high-gain.

He pulled a face that he hoped Ed would interpret as 'trust me', then reset the bug. Now it would transmit instead of receive. Holding his breath, he scraped its mike with his fingernail. With any luck at all, it would sound exactly like the noise a bugged line would make. Not that any bug of Ros's would ever fail.

There was a click and the line went dead. Not stupid then, Mr Zander. Beckett bit his lip. Everything depended on just how bright Zander was.

He picked up the phone.

Wrong answer, Zander, Beckett thought. You can't call security on a bugged line. Come on, think it through. There was a single sharp click as Zander punched a number. Then a pause. And the sound of the receiver being replaced.

Beckett realised he was holding his breath, and allowed himself the luxury of exhaling it softly.

That's it, he thought. Off you go and inform your security staff. A moment later he was rewarded with the sound of soft footsteps retreating across the carpet, and then the door opening.

Ed reached to open the cupboard door. Beckett laid a warning hand on his sleeve. He counted down mentally . . . three, two, one. He nodded.

Time to go for it. If Zander was still around, it was just too bad.

Ed cautiously opened the door. A sliver of light shafted into the gloom, then widened as the door swung open.

The room seemed empty, but the expanse of carpet between them and the door seemed as wide and threatening as the Sahara. If Zander walked back into the room now, they'd be trapped without cover.

That meant there was only one way to do this – fast and quiet. He let Ed lead the way as they dashed silently to the door.

They paused in the doorway. Zander was further down the corridor, heading towards the elevators. Damn, Beckett thought. They slipped into the corridor, then pelted down it away from Zander.

Beckett spared a glance back as they came to the first corner – just in time to see Zander also looking back.

So that was the opposition, Beckett thought as he ran after Ed. Slick, very slick – sharp black suit, grey shirt, tie the colour of blood.

– too slick, in fact. The intruder alarms began to wail for the second time that day.

They slammed through the emergency exit doors into the stairwell. Down the stairs, three at a time. Their shoes rang on the cold stone. Beckett's breath rasped harshly. They passed one set of doors. Another. Another.

He glanced up at the sign glowing above the next set of doors. Forty-ninth floor. At least they were going down.

Somewhere below them, a door slammed.

He stopped. So did Ed. As one, they peered over the banister. Stairs looped backwards and forwards, it seemed almost to infinity. Beckett squeezed his eyes shut.

He hadn't been mistaken. Security guards were pouring up the stairs. Two or a dozen, it didn't matter.

He turned and ran up the stairs. Ed was already ahead of him.

The siren whooped, two tones, rising and falling.

Going up was much harder than coming down had been. The breath jolted out of Beckett with every step, and with every step he imagined the guards getting closer.

Behind him, someone yelled. Did they shout, 'Get your hands up'? They could be armed.

Surely not.

He dismissed the idea from his thoughts and put his energy into running.

They had to get to the top of the building. That high, maybe no guards would have been set. He had to hope they'd think going up was an idea too stupid to contemplate.

As the breath burned in his throat, he thought maybe they were right.

How many more floors? Fifty-nine, said the sign above the door.

Sixty. That was a nice round number, a number an architect could relate to –

Ed flung himself through the double doors into the corridor. Beckett was just behind him.

The plain-painted walls and perforated steel floor were in stark contrast to the opulence below.

No one in sight. If it hadn't been for the siren's continuing shriek, Beckett might almost have been able to forget that they were in trouble.

But trouble was coming up the stairs behind them, and gaining with every second.

'Over there!' Ed said, pointing at an anodised steel door. Beckett followed him across to it. A sign in three-inch-high letters barred access to those without proper authorisation. 'Got your authorisation?' Ed asked.

Beckett grinned. Out came his electronic lock pick, and five seconds later he was pulling the door open.

He found himself staring out at the open sky and nothing but clouds. He felt himself falling forwards even as he realised he was looking at the top of the lift-shaft.

'Excellent!' Ed said, and jumped into it. Beckett didn't even have time to gasp before the whole shaft rang like a bell. 'You aren't scared of heights are you?' Ed's voice echoed up to him.

Beckett looked down. Ed was standing about ten feet down, on the top of the lift car. He sighed, and jumped down on to it.

Ed peered at Beckett's face for a moment, then at the gap between the car and the shaft. 'Don't look down,' he advised. He glanced out of the window. 'Don't look anywhere.'

I do *not* look frightened, Beckett thought indignantly; but there was no time to say anything. Ed reached up and closed the access door, then flipped open the service panel next to it and punched a couple of buttons.

'Nothing to it,' he said.

'Great,' Beckett said. He followed Ed's lead and held on to the static cable of the lift.

The car started to move. For a second Beckett couldn't feel anything beneath his feet. His stomach flip-flopped. Then things settled back down again. He risked a glance out of the window, and regretted it immediately.

36

He squeezed his eyes shut, then opened them slowly.

'Are you feeling all right?' Ed asked. 'You look a bit green.'

'Shut up, Ed.'

I am not going to shut my eyes, Beckett thought. He made himself look through the window at the world hurtling past.

'When we stop I'll try to open the door above,' Ed said.

Beckett nodded, glad of the distraction.

Abruptly, the lift shuddered to a halt. Ed stepped on to the ledge in front of the door and clung there while he tried to force an exit.

'Got it open yet?' Beckett asked. He was sure the building was swaying. Or maybe he was.

Before Ed could answer, the lift car started to climb. Ed hopped nimbly back on to it, and there was nothing they could do but watch the world fall away outside again.

Beckett stared up at the lift cables. They seemed to recede into infinity. What if we got to the top and just kept going? he thought. The roof could open up and we'd just keep going... then he had a worse thought. Suppose they kept going and the roof didn't open up? He and Ed would be squashed like flies. There were safety interlocks to prevent the lift going past the service hatch, but what if someone overrode them ... someone with a lot to lose, like Zander, say? He could call it an accident, say they'd been running from his security and taken out the overrides when they hijacked the lift. Beckett swallowed hard. Zander, he reasoned, wouldn't want to generate the interest their disappearance would cause. No, the worst that would happen if they got caught was that they'd be escorted firmly off the premises.

The lift slid to a halt again. There was a slight jolt

as the doors opened and someone got out.

'Caught them yet?' came a male voice.

'No, sir – they must be on the roof,' came another, slightly younger by the sound of it. 'It's been sealed off.'

Well, that was a useful piece of information, Beckett thought. At least now he had a good reason to insist they go down instead of up.

The lift moved off again. Down. At least we're going in the right direction, Beckett thought.

'There they are!' a voice shouted. 'On top of the lift!'

Beckett laid his head against the static cable. He'd never imagined he'd want it, but he wished the lift would go faster. Anything to get this over with.

The car stopped again. Ed made another attempt on the door, and this time he succeeded. He pelted out, carrying the holdall. Beckett followed him. As he got out of the lift, he staggered. The walls were too close, the floor too solid. Think about it later, he told himself as he raced after Ed.

They were on the mezzanine floor. Ed headed for the railings. Oh not that, Beckett thought. But he looked at the long, shallow curve of the stairs and knew that Ed was right. They'd never make it out before the guards got there if they took that route.

Ed got to the rail and vaulted over it. Beckett arrived a second later. He looked over. It's only ten feet, he told himself. Easy. Ed was already halfway to the door.

Beckett licked his lips. Any minute now, the guards would arrive. He clambered over the railings, hung by his hands for an instant, then let himself drop.

He landed bent-kneed, gave himself time for one long, hard breath, then ran after Ed.

Fresh air had never tasted sweeter. Footsteps pounded behind him. More than one person, he reckoned. He didn't even bother to glance back, just forced an extra burst of speed out of his complaining muscles until he reached the car.

Ed already had the engine running. He threw himself into the passenger seat; Ed had the car in motion before he'd even shut the door. In the rear-view mirror, he saw the guards chasing uselessly after them and grinned.

Someone was watching Ros as she worked. She could feel the presence of the other person – the sound of breathing, the shadow cast across the computer screen. She tapped in one last command, and glanced up. Sally was standing right next to her. Ros hadn't even heard her approach.

'What are you doing?' Sally asked. She perched on the desk to watch.

'The alarm on the door that was left open is computer-operated,' Ros said. She pressed the 'enter' key, and a message telling her that her infiltration program had been launched appeared on the screen.

'Oh?' Sally said. She didn't seem to follow.

Typical specialist, Ros thought. Give her a bio-engineering problem to investigate and she'd think of ten ways to tackle it in as many seconds; confront her with anything outside that and she was lost.

'It had to be accessed with a personal user ID – whoever did it has wiped all the records,' she went on. Sally nodded. 'But I'm running a little program of my own to recover them.' She tapped the screen, where a bar showed the percentage of the computer server's hard disk that had been infiltrated and checked.

'Nice work,' Sally said. She grinned, and Ros realised that the Gizmos team had just gone up in her estimation. That was excellent – Sally probably knew as much about what was going on as Lennox did, and certainly more than Glass. She might come in very useful, if she thought they were worth helping.

Ros tapped a few keys to make the computer switch tasks. 'Meanwhile, I'm more interested in trying to read this Fricker file that Lennox is so keen to hide.' She loaded her second infiltration program, and set up its parameters. That took a few minutes of concentrated work, so she was glad that Sally didn't bother her with more questions.

Once the program was running, she asked, 'Sally, did you know Fricker?' There was no answer. 'Sally?' She looked round. Sally had gone. Ros spun round the other way in her chair. The monitoring station Sally had been using was vacant.

Ros scowled at the computer. Her program beeped to let her know that it had overcome Lennox's security measures. Damn, she thought. Maybe Sally had decided to let Lennox know what she was doing.

She got up hurriedly and started to follow the other woman, but before she got very far a movement on one of the screens monitoring the Propagation Chamber caught her eye. Sally was hurrying down the chamber wearing a breathing mask and with something heavy in her hands.

Must be something wrong, Ros thought. She was surprised she hadn't noticed the monitoring station beeping, but she had to admit that she'd been pretty bound up in her work – Ed had once said she wouldn't notice a bomb going off under her chair if she were working on a programming problem.

The monitor went blank.

Ros tapped at the buttons on it, but the screen stayed blank. Just then the other monitors started to bleep urgently. Ros turned. The same message, written in inch-high letters, was flashing on every screen: ALERT – PROPAGATION CHAMBER FAILURE.

Well, that's informative, Ros thought. She hurried over to the intercom and flipped it on. 'Sally, are you all right?'

No answer.

Ros crossed the control area to the door of the Propagation Suite and punched in the ID number she'd been given. She pulled open the heavy steel door and went through.

'Sally?' she called, but the room was empty.

Ros's eyes widened as she realised the outer door of the airlock was standing open. No wonder the alarms had gone off.

A single breathing mask hung by it. She examined it quickly, then slung the cylinder across her shoulder and fitted the mask over her mouth and nose.

She went into the airlock and started the cycle. When the 'ready' light went on, she opened the inner door and went through cautiously. Whatever had happened to Sally might be about to happen to her.

Flat tanks of algae stretched out in front of her as far as she could see. They gave an eerie, greenish quality to the flat white light, an effect that was enhanced by the bubbling sounds the water filters made, and the hiss of the atmosphere control plant.

'Sally?' The mask made Ros's voice sound echoey and strange.

She couldn't see the other woman anywhere, so she started to walk down the central aisle.

This is stupid, she thought. What if there's another intruder? Far smarter to call security, let them deal with the heavy physical stuff.

But it probably wasn't that. It was probably just a minor equipment failure. Sally was probably working under one of the tanks somewhere, which would explain why Ros hadn't yet spotted her.

Though what could be so urgent as to make her

leave the outer door open, Ros couldn't think.

A sound behind her made her turn, just in time to see a flash of white disappearing through the airlock. The door clanged shut. Ros felt the impact of metal on metal vibrate through the floor even through its rubberised surface.

She walked back, wondering how Sally had missed seeing her, and pulled the doorhandle. The heavy steel bar refused to move.

Blast, she thought. Sally must have locked up behind her. Bad working practice, she thought. Bad security, come to that – a place like this should only be locked off once the building was clear. Still, at least they'd installed a proper alarm system.

She punched the button next to the door. Nothing happened. She tried it again. This time a message flashed up on its LCD read-out: 'System Offline for Maintenance. Please Try Again Later.'

It was too much of a coincidence, Ros realised. Well, she thought, I wanted to know who the traitor is, and now I do. Who better to act the mole than Lennox's right-hand woman?

She felt her pulse start to race. Keep calm, she thought. I could be wrong – it might not be Sally. Any minute now, she'll realise what's happened and come to release me. But she knew that was just the panic talking. Think of another alternative, then, she told herself. There's always another alternative.

She ran back down to the end of the chamber, to where the security camera panned back and forth. She waved her arms at it. Someone had to be watching. If not Sally, then Glass, or Lennox himself.

It was only when the camera moved through the extreme angle of its pan that she spotted the wires that had been cut and pushed neatly back out of sight.

Now the panic threatened to engulf her. She felt her

pulse hammer at her wrists and temples, heard her breath rasping in the breathing mask.

The mask . . . she glanced down at the meter on the cylinder. A red LED flashed at her. FIVE MINUTES said the time remaining display.

Ros let the cylinder fall from her hand with a mixture of rage and fear.

The blind eye of the lens swung back to confront her, as if to mock her terror.

Sally moved round the control area, putting the screens on the environment monitors into stand-by mode.

It would never do for someone to come along and see them screaming out their alert – at least, not while she was still there and that too-clever-by-half security consultant was still alive.

She thought for a moment, then went to her monitoring station. The oxygen level in the Propagation Chamber was currently at the maximum safe level for the Phodex. Sally reached out and touched the control. She hesitated for a moment longer, then punched it. The LED showing the required level dropped to minimum. The indicator displaying the actual level started to drop slowly to match it.

Thinking of which, she had one more thing to do before she left. She walked over to the computer station Ros had been using. The infiltration programs had done their job.

Sally ignored the one that had reconstructed the door log. She didn't need it: after all, she already knew who had let Zander's raiding party in – no one knew better, in fact.

It was the result of the other program that interested her. She never had been able to coax Lennox into telling her what had killed James Fricker, but she was about to find out. And she and Zander would find a way to make it pay.

She downloaded the results onto a floppy disk, then erased the originals. No doubt Ms Clever-clever could have reconstructed them – but she wasn't going to be around to try.

Serve her right.

Sally slipped the disk into the pocket of her lab coat, and left the control area. At the door, she turned and looked back. She wasn't going to miss the place at all, she decided.

No, she thought as she made her way quickly to the front exit – missing people and places was weak, for weak people. Weak people were losers – poor people who stayed poor, and never tasted everything life had to offer.

She would. She would be stinking rich, and no one was going to stop her.

As she walked through the building, the lights switched themselves off behind her, so that she walked from the darkness to the light.

She liked that image.

Just as she thought she'd got clean away, she heard Lennox call her name.

She glanced up. He was standing on the mezzanine floor, leaning on the railing. He'd once told her it made him feel like a king surveying his kingdom. She'd smiled and said something complimentary about it suiting him: but inside she'd seethed. What was he – a second-rate little scientist, looking out over his third-rate company and congratulating himself because it wasn't fourth-rate? Worse, he'd never offered her a Christmas bonus, much less a profit share.

Well, she thought as she squinted up into the light at him, he was going to pay the price of his meanness now.

'All well?' he asked.

'Yes,' Sally said, and was appalled at how nervous she sounded. 'Yes,' she said again, more firmly. 'I'm off now.' Lennox stared at her. Only he was ever allowed to leave before seven: he considered anything less a sign of lack of commitment. He'll never know how much I lack commitment, Sally thought: but she managed to keep the smile off her face. 'That girl – Ros?' she added. 'She's gone.' Lennox's eyebrows rose. She knew what he was thinking – that for what he was paying them, she should have been there till midnight. That always was his problem – he didn't think of anything but money. 'Hairdressers, she said,' Sally finished.

Lennox pulled a sour face. 'Goodnight then,' he said.

'Goodnight,' Sally replied. And goodbye, she thought. She left the building, and this time she didn't look back.

Pain.

Ros panted with the effort of trying to drag enough oxygen into her starving lungs even as panic closed her throat. She stared round wildly.

Death surely couldn't come so easily. There had to be something she could do. She spotted a sampling net hanging on the wall.

Break the glass in the door with it? Maybe.

Got to be worth the effort of trying. But the more she moved, the more oxygen she used. Never mind. There was almost no oxygen left now.

Stupid to die now. Beckett would come. Ed would come. She had to hang on. Let them know where she was.

It took all her willpower not to rip the suffocating mask from her face, and to begin to stagger across the chamber to the net.

But she did it.

* * *

Ed swung the off-road vehicle into the parking bay in front of the New Earth Foods building.

Nothing like a bit of a chase to get the old adrenalin pumping, he thought. Pity Zander's lot hadn't tried harder, really. He grinned, thinking how he could embroider their little escapade when he told Ros about it.

Then he glanced at Beckett's face, and his grin died.

'Well, that was a fiasco,' Beckett said. 'We didn't get the computer bug in place, Zander probably knows we've bugged his phones, and he definitely knows we're on to him.'

'Let's hope Ros is having better luck,' Ed said.

Little breaths. *Little* breaths. Yet she wanted to gulp at the air.

The room swam in front of her. She reached the net. Grabbed at it. Missed.

Again.

Got it.

The door . . . the door was so far away. And the glass was reinforced anyway.

She stared at the red glass. At the red alarm.

Alarm system offline. Sally did that. All Sally's fault.

Ros's ears buzzed. She was going to die here. All Sally's fault.

Alarm system offline for maintenance. Please try again later.

But now was later. Little breaths. Sip at the air. Not gulp.

She had to think. Alarm systems. Phodex would only kill you if you fell in the tank. Stupid idea. Fall in the tank.

Something picked at her brain. Flashing lights. Where had she seen . . . on the screens. Other monitors. Other alarms.

Good. But how to set them off? Intruder alert, fire alarm – stupid, no oxygen for fire, electrical fault.

That was it. She hefted the sampling net. So heavy. Like her arms, like her legs. Break the tanks? Steel. Not good for breaking.

But the lights . . . She slashed at them with the pole.

Chest hurt. Arms like lead. Never mind. Just do it.

The pole swished through the air. Crash, it went, into the light tube. Bits of glass sparkling in the white light . . .

Ros fell forward. Please, she thought, and thought nothing more.

The New Earth Foods building was almost deserted when Ed and Beckett reached the front entrance. Only the security lights in the lobby showed that anyone at all was still there.

Ed pushed open the glass door, and a rush of warmer air met him. Lennox was waiting for them.

'How did you get on?' he asked.

'Badly,' Beckett said. Anger was written in every line of his face.

'What –' Lennox started.

'Who else knew we were going to Hennessey-Brock?' Ed cut in. Stupid questions would only irritate Beckett and waste everyone's time.

'Mr Glass,' Lennox said. 'Myself – and Sally, of course.'

Well, that probably explained their mysterious lady caller, Ed thought, then chided himself for jumping to conclusions – anyone who was really good with a distortion unit could easily have changed the apparent gender of their voice.

While he was still pondering that, Beckett said, 'And where is Sally now?'

'She was helping your colleague, but they've both

47

gone for the night,' Lennox said.

'Ros has gone?' Ed said. He glanced at Beckett. The expression on his face said he was just as surprised – especially when Ros had a whole new computer network to play with. And she'd specifically told them she would meet them here.

'To the hairdresser's, apparently,' Lennox said.

'And I'm a little green man from Mars,' Ed said. He strode off without waiting for Beckett to follow him.

She had said she was going to be working in the Phodex Propagation Suite. Ed had only been there once, but he never forgot directions. He threaded his way through the open-plan offices, with the lights flicking on ahead of him. The more he thought about it, the more worried he got and the faster he walked. Behind him, he could just make out the soft sounds of Beckett's footsteps on the rubberised flooring; and somewhere behind those, Lennox huffing and puffing to keep up.

Too bad. There was a cold knot in the pit of Ed's stomach. How many ways could you kill someone in a laboratory? And how long might it take?

Ahead of him, the Propagation Suite control area opened out. Ranks of monitors cast a bluish glow in the darkness, as messages scrolled up their screens.

Warning messages in inch-high letters.

Ed broke into a dead run.

As he entered the control area, the overhead lighting switched itself on. The whole place was deserted.

No dead bodies. That was something.

He looked round. Ros's jacket and holdall were by one of the workstations. He saw Lennox staring at him.

'That's Ros's kit,' he said, just to make sure the other man got the point. 'Where the hell is she?'

Lennox stared at him blankly. There's no one so stupid as a man who thinks he's a genius, Ed decided.

'What's this?' Beckett said. 'Lighting failure.' He pointed to one of the screens.

'It just means a bulb has gone,' Lennox said.

Ask that man the time of day and he'd answer like you were accusing him of murder, Ed thought.

'Well it says the whole circuit's gone –' Beckett snapped.

'In my Propagation Chamber?' Lennox said. 'It can't . . .'

This time it was Beckett who left at a dead run, and Ed who followed him. As they got to the Propagation Chamber, Lennox pushed past. He tapped something into a keypad by the door.

'What are you doing?' Ed asked.

'Cycling the airlock,' Lennox said. 'It'll only take a mo–'

'Override it,' Beckett said.

Lennox glared at them.

If he mentions his Phodex, I'll thump him, Ed thought. 'Do it,' he said.

Lennox punched in another code. Even before he had finished, Beckett was leaning on the handle. The door swung in. Ed held it while Beckett opened the inner door.

Ros was sprawled a few metres inside the chamber. Ed took a deep breath and ran in to get her. At that, he was only just ahead of Beckett.

'There's no oxygen,' Lennox called from the safety of the doorway. 'Get her out.'

She didn't seem to be breathing. Ed forced himself not to check her pulse. Get her out first, everything else comes second.

He started to drag her; then with Beckett's help, he got her into a fireman's lift.

Can't feel her breathing, he thought as he stepped across the lip of the airlock door. Would I be able to? He didn't know.

'Oxygen,' he heard Beckett say. 'We need oxygen.'

He laid her down gently on the floor of the control area. Her skin was the colour of putty, rather than its usual café au lait, and her lips and cheeks were bloodless.

He loosened her collar and checked her mouth for obstructions, then covered her mouth with his own. Breathed out. Counted . . .

A hand thrust something at him. He ignored it.

'Oxygen,' said a voice.

Breathed out, breathed life into her.

'Ed,' Beckett said urgently. 'Oxygen.'

Ed looked round. Lennox was offering him a breathing mask. He took it. His hands were shaking. Oxygen hissed through the gas-line.

He put it over her mouth and nose. 'Ros, breathe for me . . .' he pleaded. Just a breath or two. If he'd floored the accelerator a bit harder on the way back . . . If he hadn't wasted time on sarcasm, pointing out her kit to Lennox . . . If he . . .

Ros coughed. Her chest spasmed, and her hand clawed at the mask. Her eyes fluttered open.

'Excellent!' Ed said. He smoothed her hair back from her face. It was all he could do to stop himself punching the air in exultation.

There was a moment in which none of them spoke.

Then Beckett said, 'Sally, yes?'

Ros nodded weakly.

Ed glared at Lennox. 'It certainly brings out the worst in people, this pondweed of yours,' he said.

50

« Four »

Rafael D'Angelo stepped out of the lift on the thirty-sixth floor of the Sci-Technicon Hotel. Dawn was just beginning to break, and pale sunlight filtered through the wall-high windows of the corridor.

D'Angelo's feet made no sound in the thick pile carpet as he searched for room 3605. He found it quickly, and paused for a moment outside the door.

He took a small bell-shaped device from his pocket and pressed its larger end to the beaten copper of the door. He put his ear to the other end, and listened. The only sound he could hear was the quiet susurration of one person's breath.

D'Angelo never smiled. But he came close now.

He glanced round, then took a second device from his pocket. This one looked like a standard credit card. He wiped it through the magnetic strip-reader in the door lock. There was a quiet click as the door opened.

Sometimes the simplest methods were the best. The hotel staff had been remarkably easy to bribe.

D'Angelo withdrew his gun from his pocket. He slipped inside the room and shut the door behind him. The room was shadowy, with only a minimum of light straggling through the closed blinds. Various bits of equipment lay scattered on the flat surfaces all around the room.

D'Angelo went and sat on the edge of the bed.

He laid the gun next to Stross's ear. 'Wake up, Doctor Stross,' he said. 'But please don't make any sudden movements.'

Stross's eyes flicked open. 'Wha?' he said.

'You have something I want,' D'Angelo said. 'Get up, get dressed, and pack the equipment you demonstrated yesterday. Do it now and do it silently, or your use to me will be at an end.' Stross didn't move. 'Do you understand me?' D'Angelo asked.

'Yes,' Stross said. He was clearly still waking up. 'Just give me a couple of minutes.'

'You don't have a couple of minutes, Doctor Stross – you have thirty seconds, counting from now.'

Stross scrambled up. It was obvious the danger of his situation had finally sunk in. He was clearly terrified. That pleased D'Angelo. Heroes were so utterly tedious.

'What now?' Stross asked.

'Get the sound neutraliser you demonstrated in your lecture,' D'Angelo said. Stross nodded. He pulled a case from under his bed, and started to pack equipment into it. His hands were shaking. On second thoughts, D'Angelo thought, cowards could be just as tedious. 'Also the other equipment, and all your clothes.' Stross turned to him. 'Don't ask,' D'Angelo said. 'You don't want to know the answer.'

A few minutes later, he was marching Stross through the lobby. The man had his instructions: check out, saying he was unwell, or discover the pleasures of a bullet in the cerebellum.

He followed them to the letter.

Together, they left the hotel. At that time of the

morning, the streets were deserted. They walked two blocks to an underground car park where D'Angelo – looking quite different – had left a car several days previously on long-term stay.

The car was very fast but totally nondescript.

'Get in, Doctor Stross,' D'Angelo said. 'You're driving.'

As Stross turned to open the door, D'Angelo slammed the butt of the gun into his head. Stross crumpled to the floor. Swiftly D'Angelo cuffed his wrists behind him, blindfolded him, and taped his mouth shut. Manhandling him into the boot of the car took a little longer.

D'Angelo slammed the lid shut, and drove off slowly enough not to attract attention.

Phase one complete, he thought.

Zander was not a happy man.

He strode through the Hennessey-Brock building, acknowledging the greetings of his staff with the merest nod of his head. He knew his fury must be evident in his eyes, in the set of his jaw. His underlings did not speak to him. They knew better, he thought with some satisfaction: those who did not had long since moved to positions with other, less demanding companies.

A lesser man might have allowed his spirits to be lifted by the morning sun shafting through the blued glass of the building's windows, or by the excellent coffee and pastries provided for breakfast. A lesser man might have presumed that everything would work out for the best in the end. A lesser man might have assumed that his original plans would still win through.

Zander did none of these things. Instead, as he pushed open his office door he was already adjusting his plans, deciding where he could obtain the staff and information he would need for a renewed assault on New Earth Foods, one using entirely new strategies that Lennox would be unable to predict or counter.

His desk, as befitted that of a truly superior man – one who knew how to delegate – was bare. Behind it stood his high-backed leather chair, facing towards the window and out over the city, spread out so far below the Hennessey-Brock tower.

There was something odd. He paused, trying to figure it out. A noise? A reflection in the glass? Something.

The chair swung round. Sally smiled at him. She was beautiful, intelligent and they had much in common.

Consequently he didn't trust her in the least.

'What are you doing here?' he demanded.

'I need to talk to you,' she said. She smiled a tiny, catlike smile that he had once found most attractive.

'The raid was a failure,' he said. He did not find incompetence attractive in the least. 'Get out of my chair – you're fired.'

Sally didn't move. 'That wasn't my fault,' she said. 'And I did tell you about those security people.' She pouted. That pout had once had the power to put anything else out of his mind. No more.

Zander crossed to the desk and opened the top drawer. The smell of her perfume was subtle, yet unmissable. But nothing he couldn't ignore. He pulled out the bug it had taken his own security staff so long to track down. 'You didn't stop them planting this, though, did you?' he demanded. Sally smiled. 'Get out,' he said.

For an answer, she pulled a disk out of her jacket pocket. 'Things have changed,' she said. She got up, making it clear she was doing it in her own time. The reflection of her orange jacket and black dress made shimmering, abstract patterns in the windows. 'I've discovered something.' She held the disk up between her hands and leant forward, tantalising him.

'The formula for Phodex?' It was more than he'd hoped for – not more than he'd dreamed of, but more than he'd ever expected to get without a great deal of work. And now here Sally was, tempting him with it.

'Better than that,' she said. Zander scowled. 'Something we can use to bring Lennox to his knees . . .' She let her voice trail off. Vindictive little cat, Zander thought. She laid her hand on his cheek. 'You see, I've discovered that Phodex is deeply flawed.' She shook her head, all mock seriousness: the sun sparked copper in her dark hair. Zander felt his heart thundering in his chest. 'Under the right circumstances, it . . . well, let's just say you wouldn't want to eat it after all.'

'Then it's useless,' Zander said. He felt his castles in the air go tumbling down around him. 'If it's useless to New Earth Foods, it's just as useless to Hennessey-Brock . . .'

Sally laid her finger on his mouth. She tasted of lemons and salt. 'Oh Zander, you just aren't thinking, are you?' She smiled, that secretive little cat smile he never had been able to penetrate. 'Suppose we had stolen the Phodex formula? You'd have marketed it. But so would Lennox: it might have taken him a while, but he'd have recreated his work –'

'But we'd have had the patents . . .' Zander protested.

Anger flashed in Sally's eyes. 'Maybe – but would you have wanted to try and enforce them in law? And at best – at *best* you'd have had a marketing war on your hands.' She fiddled with his shirt buttons. 'But there's another way. A way with more immediate gains . . . if you'll just follow my suggestions.' She looked up at him. Chewed her bottom lip. Bestowed a hint of a smile on him. 'The rewards could be . . . well,

I'm sure you can imagine the rewards.' She came and sat on the table, letting her dress ride up, revealing what seemed like yards of black-clad thigh. 'The first thing we should do is put Lennox under some pressure. Don't you think?' She leant forward.

Zander found that his mouth had gone quite dry. He nodded.

The headquarters Rafael D'Angelo had chosen for his current operation had once been a laboratory developing supersaturated long-chain hydrocarbons: fuel oils that would burn eight or ten times as long as normal. That had been years ago, and the energy industry had moved on.

Now the laboratory stood in a deserted industrial park on the edge of the city. Its squat, box-like shape was lent grace by several towers and a central dome, and its walls were clad in white enamelled steel. As D'Angelo approached it through the early morning mist, it seemed almost ghostly.

He pulled up in front of it, and hauled the cuffed, gagged and panicking Charles Stross out of the boot of his car. He pushed the man along in front of him, keeping his pistol jammed just behind his jawbone the whole time with one hand. With the other he carried the case containing the Stross Cybertech equipment.

The room he had selected as Stross's prison was quite near the entrance, but hidden in a maze of corridors. The door was made of brushed steel, with a smoked glass observation panel set into it. He pulled down the handle, and it swung slowly open.

The room had been a test chamber of some kind, D'Angelo reckoned. It was windowless and steel-clad. A couple of large tables were bolted to the floor, but otherwise it was completely bare. Flat white light came from a ring illuminator set flush into the ceiling, and bounced endlessly off the walls.

He put the case down and shoved Stross hard. The man stumbled forward, straight into one of the tables. Winded, he doubled over. After a moment he struggled upright. The panic was still in his eyes, but it was muted now.

In the case of fear, D'Angelo thought, familiarity breeds content.

That would never do.

He aimed the pistol at Stross. 'Understand me, Doctor Stross,' he said. 'I have no real need of you. You are alive only because I may need you to explain some of your equipment. Do you understand?' Stross nodded. His skin was pallid against the black halo of his hair. 'However, it all seems most straightforward – so if you give me any trouble, you will be dead very shortly afterwards. Do you understand *that*?'

Again, Stross nodded.

D'Angelo stepped backwards out of the room. He swung the door shut and lowered the pistol. A single jerk on the handle locked the door.

He slipped the pistol back into his jacket pocket, picked up the precious equipment, and set off for the room he had put aside for himself.

It occupied the whole of one of the smaller domes, at the very top of one of the highest towers. The dome was made of transparent glass, so that it was possible to look out in any direction.

Though he'd been using it on and off for a couple of weeks, it was almost as sparsely furnished as the cubicle where he'd left Stross. There was nothing to personalise it, just a pallet on the floor, a mirror on the table by the sink and two large suitcases. One held his clothes. The other was tamper-proof, security-probe-proof, and full of weapons and equipment.

D'Angelo put the case containing the Stross Cyber-tech equipment down. The job he was doing for his present client, Raymond Charlesworth, required only the sound suppressor. The rest he regarded as a bonus.

There was just time for D'Angelo to prepare for the demonstration. He took a small black bottle and a rather larger canister from his equipment case, and went over to the mirror.

He squirted blue foam from the canister, and applied it to his face. He waited for a moment, then began to claw at his face with his nails.

His flesh peeled away, at first in small pieces and then in large lumps. He threw the resulting mess into the sink and ran hot water on it. It dissolved and drained away.

D'Angelo ran his fingers over his face. The last traces of the dermaplastic pulled away. He pulled the blond wig off, and looked at himself in the mirror.

The only reminders of the blond man were his bright blue eyes and blond eyebrows. Otherwise, the man looking at D'Angelo was mousy-haired and thin-faced, absolutely nondescript. He rubbed liquid from the bottle into his eyebrows and they peeled away. He popped out his blue contact lenses, revealing his own, almost colour-less irises beneath them. Now his face was a blank, a mere canvas for what he would impose upon it.

He went back to his bag and got out a large tube and a flat box. From the tube he squirted fresh derma-plastic, which he mixed with pigments from the box. Deftly, he began to apply the mixture to his face, working first quite crudely, then smoothing down the dermaplastic and adding tinier and tinier amounts until he was satisfied with the effect. He chose a picture from a selection in his bag and compared it to his face. A few minute adjustments later, he was satisfied. He added a dark wig and matching eyebrows. Finally, he put a pair of mirrored contact lenses into his eyes.

He looked at himself. A heavy-set, swarthy man looked back at him. Images reflected in his eyes, smaller and smaller downward to infinity, till they were not there at all.

The clothes came next. He took off D'Angelo's designer suit, and put on jeans, an open-necked shirt and a leather jacket carefully padded to make him look broader than he was, all in black.

He pulled out the driving licence he had been carrying. He threw it in the sink, squirted more of the derma-solvent on it, and set it alight. Fire gouted up for a second or two, and there was a brief plume of white smoke.

'Goodbye, Mr D'Angelo,' he said aloud. 'Welcome back, Mr Da Silva.'

Ros wrapped her hands round her mug of tea and sipped at it. Seven-thirty in the morning. Not her favourite time of day, but Lennox's message had been urgent, so she, Ed and Beckett had hurried over to his office.

Beckett stared at Lennox's computer screen. 'Cancel the launch. We know the secret of Phodex,' he read.

The screen flickered as the message repeated and scrolled up the screen. According to Lennox, it had been doing that ever since he logged on that morning – and it was on every machine on New Earth Foods' internal network, stopping all other electronic communication in and out.

'Outrageous,' Lennox said, jabbing a finger at the computer. 'What a nerve Zander's got.'

'What does he mean?' Beckett asked. 'The secret of Phodex?'

Ros was more than willing to let him do the talking, just this once.

'The formula, of course,' Lennox said. Ros frowned. He was just a little too quick with that. He turned to her. 'How are you feeling today?' His face was a picture of concern. Slimy so-and-so, Ros thought. She was beginning to realise that she didn't like him very much at all.

'Getting there,' she admitted, hoping she didn't look as tired as she felt. What little sleep she had managed had been broken by nightmares she remembered only as scattered, frightening images.

'Is it just the formula?' Ed asked. Ros was glad to see the others weren't about to let Lennox change the subject. 'Or is there something about Phodex we should know?'

Time to pitch in, Ros thought. Nightmares were one thing. The job was quite another. 'Why the cover-up over the man who died?' She was gratified to see the indignant look on Lennox's face. Time to push him a bit further than he'd like to go. 'Did that involve Phodex?'

'There is no cover-up,' Lennox said. 'Phodex is absolutely safe.'

Ros shifted in her seat a bit, to get a better look at him. Methinks the gentleman doth protest too much, she thought. She glanced at Beckett, and saw from his expression that he obviously thought much the same.

'So what now?' she asked, making sure her voice was as unthreatening as possible. 'Will you cancel the launch party?'

'Certainly not,' Lennox shouted. He took a deep breath, and made an obvious effort to moderate his tone. 'It's my life's work.' More to the point, Ros thought, he'd spent close on half a million on the launch, what with promotional videos, a press campaign, flying in representatives of interested countries and aid organisations – no, she could see how he wouldn't want to call all that off. He paced to and fro across the office, then halted next to the computer. 'Whatever Zander and that wretched girl are planning, I want you to ensure they fail.'

'And how do you want us to do that?' Ros asked, though in her experience the client was the last person to have any idea how security ought to be carried out.

'The Phodex will be at its most vulnerable when we move it between New Earth Foods and The Green Machine –'

'The restaurant you're using for the launch?' Ed asked.

Lennox nodded. 'I want you to supervise transportation of the Phodex.'

Oh good, Ros thought. She loved driving.

Joseph Da Silva – Rafael D'Angelo, as he had been – met Raymond Charlesworth in one of the vast test chambers that lay at the bottom of the laboratories.

The man was, Da Silva thought, like all his kind: a besuited, juiceless, frightened mouse of a man who would die without ever really having lived.

But that was all right: Charlesworth would readily pay Da Silva to do what he lacked the guts and the wits to do for himself.

He led Charlesworth to the back of the test chamber, where he had arranged the demonstration. A number of silver hemispheres half as tall as he was were bolted to the floor. Da Silva had placed a large cube of polymer-coated brick in each one. He produced two flat packages, each with an infra-red detector attached to it, from the suitcase he had left near the hemispheres.

'MDX,' he said, holding them up. Charlesworth blanched and stepped back. Fool, Da Silva thought. The explosive was perfectly safe unless the detonator was triggered. 'Choose one,' he said.

61

Charlesworth pointed to the package in his left hand. Da Silva went and attached it to the left-hand cube, then returned to Charlesworth.

'Is this safe?' Charlesworth asked.

'What's the matter? Don't you trust me?' Da Silva asked. He turned his silvered gaze on Charlesworth. The man looked away. 'It's as safe as explosives ever are, and the polymer coating will stop ricochets.' Charlesworth smiled nervously. 'Still, I'd step back a bit,' Da Silva said. It was always best to keep them off-guard.

They retreated a bit further. Da Silva pointed the trigger at the cube. There was a flash and a dull whump, and the cube disintegrated into a pile of chips. The polymer flared briefly, and then there was nothing but a rapidly dispersing cloud of smoke.

'There,' he said to Charlesworth. 'That wasn't so bad, was it?'

Charlesworth shook his head.

Da Silva went and attached the MDX to the remaining block, then came back and set up the sound suppressor he had liberated from Stross Cybertech. 'Ready?' he asked.

Without waiting for an answer, he triggered the detonator. This time the block exploded in total silence. Da Silva turned to Charlesworth and raised his eyebrows.

'That should do,' Charlesworth said.

'You know my fee.'

For the first time, Charlesworth seemed alive. 'Get me my R6 and I'll double it,' he said.

Da Silva nodded curtly. 'Tomorrow night,' he said. 'Just stick to what we arranged and everything will be fine.'

He turned and walked away, leaving Charlesworth to find his own way out.

* * *

Zander leant forward on the safety rail of the *Cloud Nine*, the restaurant he had chosen as a convenient place to keep an eye on New Earth Foods. He raised his binoculars to his eyes. The ultra-telephoto lenses whirred almost silently as they focused on his objective – the New Earth Foods building. As he watched, three men were putting large yellow containers into the back of a blood-red van. He looked at the number plate, and the eye-controlled focusing system shifted to sharpen up the digits.

He spoke into his mobile phone. 'Target is red van, registration number GZM 52.'

The mercenary he had hired acknowledged the message. He felt a hand on his shoulder.

'Won't be long now,' Sally said. He felt her nails through the silk of his shirt. She took the binoculars out of his hands. The mid-morning sun struck copper from her hair. 'Damn!' she said. 'That bloody woman is still around.' Zander stroked the creamy skin on the back of her hand. Not a woman who liked to be thwarted, Sally. She pulled her hand away impatiently. 'Looks like they're taking precautions,' she said.

Zander grabbed the binoculars back. It looked as if more cases were being brought from inside. He flipped the phone open without taking his eyes off the New Earth Foods building. 'Stand by to acquire new target car,' he said. Then, to Sally, 'See – I told you there was no need for anything more complicated.'

There was no response.

He lowered the binoculars and looked round.

Sally had gone.

Ros watched as Glass's staff loaded the crates of Phodex into the boot of her car. Ed had already left in a decoy van – a Gizmos special. Ros had done things to the engine that racing mechanics would have died to know, but Zander and his friends would never suspect it just from looking at it. If anything, it appeared so slow and clunky they'd be more likely to think it was armoured.

As for the real transport, Beckett had wanted to take his car, but it was slower and less manoeuvrable than Ros's. Besides, she thought, it would have given him a good reason for being allowed to drive.

It was amazing how much better she had felt once the prospect of a bit of driving had been mentioned. She smiled at Glass. He nodded to her, and carried on punching the crate numbers into his palmtop computer as they were carried out. He hadn't intended to, until Beckett had suggested that keeping a check on material as it left and arrived was a good idea.

Ros might almost have thought Zander had planted two moles – one for them to find, and one to remain behind. He was certainly bright enough, by all accounts. She had discounted it, though: surely no one could pretend to be as stupid as Glass.

'Any sign of company?' Beckett said into his radio headset. Ros raised her eyebrows at him. He shook his head. 'Ed says there's nothing doing.'

Ros grinned. A nice fast drive – just the thing to start the day. 'Come on then,' she said. 'Let's get going.'

She went down the few steps to the car.

'Drive carefully, sir,' Glass said to Beckett.

Ros turned and smiled at him sweetly. 'I always do,' she said.

Glass gawped at her. She opened the driver's side door.

'She's just passed her test,' Beckett whispered, so loud he must have meant for her to hear.

You'll pay for that later, she thought, and got in.

She swung out into the traffic. There was plenty of it about. That could make it harder to spot a tail. Easier to lose though. All in all, Ros wasn't unhappy with the situation.

After a few minutes, Ed radioed in. 'Still quiet here,' he said. 'Maybe the threat was a bluff?'

'Maybe,' Ros said, though she couldn't see the logic in that – it had been too non-specific to be a diversion and –

Beckett touched her arm. He pointed to the rear-view mirror. A black off-road vehicle was sitting on their tail.

'Been there long?'

'A while,' Beckett said. 'Might not be our friends, though –'

'Let's find out, shall we?'

Ros pumped the accelerator. She cut in front of the white saloon just ahead of them, then boosted through an amber traffic light. Without signalling, she cut left.

The black car was still with her.

'Can't you lose them?' Beckett demanded.

'Of course,' Ros said. 'But you're paying for the respray.'

She hung a sharp right, then another. If that's Zander, she thought, he's good. More likely, he knew where to spend his money. She smiled. Time to try a trick she'd thought of a while ago, but never had the chance to put into practice.

'You still got that present Charlie sent us?' she asked.

Beckett nodded. 'Taking the scenic route?'

'Why not?' Ros glanced in the mirror. The ORV was still with them.

She slammed through a series of turns that took them heading out of the city. The other vehicle clung to them all the way.

Ahead of them, the dark mouth of the river under-pass beckoned, barred by the horizontal shaft of its toll gate. Beckett leant out of the window, and pointed the SID at the tollgate control box at the side of the road.

The gate lifted. Ros floored the accelerator. The car roared towards the bar. Going to hit it, Ros thought. She forced herself to keep her hands on the steering wheel. All she could see was the white line of the bar, rising slowly ... surely too slowly ... but it jerked up and they were clear of it.

Beckett did something with the SID, but Ros was too busy concentrating on the road ahead to take much notice.

There was a sickening crunch from behind them. Ros glanced in the mirror. The tollgate had crashed down on the back of the pursuit vehicle.

Good enough, Ros thought. She allowed herself the luxury of a deep breath out.

The flat-bottomed cylinder of the tunnel snaked out ahead of them: bands of white ceramic alternating with brushed chrome arching overhead, and all of it illuminated by stark white tube lights.

'Don't slow down, Ros,' Beckett said.

Ros frowned. She glanced back. The black car was coming at them again, despite its crumpled back end. She accelerated a little, wanting to keep something in reserve. Wouldn't hurt if they underestimated her, either.

Light glinted silver off metal and glass. 'Looks to me very like a gun,' Ros said, and was proud of how cool she sounded.

'What?' Beckett asked. He looked back. 'Right,' he said.

A rattle of gunfire echoed through the tunnel. Ros ducked. She looked round wildly. More shots, and now she saw sparks fly, gold in the hard white light. She swerved into the oncoming lane. Back, into her own. Anything to stop them sighting.

Out again.

Floored the accelerator, and now the bands of white and chrome were flashing past.

Shots ricocheted off the walls.

'Look out!' Beckett screamed.

Lights reflected off the tunnel side. Half a heartbeat later, a road-train snaked round the corner, its electric motor silent even in the echoing cavern of the tunnel. They careened towards it. At the last moment Ros jerked the steering wheel and hauled the car back into her own lane. The black car followed her into the cavern formed by the towering side of the road-train and the curve of the tunnel. There was no room to manoeuvre, nothing to do but get past it as fast as she could. If they decided to start shooting . . . she glanced up at the side of the road-train: its blue metallic surface was painted with hazardous materials signs. FLAM-MABLE, she saw as she went past.

With luck, that would stop the gun-play; but she thought she might be running out of luck.

'Got to get out where there are more people,' she said to Beckett. He nodded grimly. Zander might be obsessed but he probably wouldn't try anything in public.

Ros floored the accelerator, trusting to skill and judgement to get her safely round the smooth curves of the tunnel. She'd counted three segments to the road-train. That should be the last – and the end of the tunnel couldn't be far off.

They barrelled round a curve, and the road opened out in front of her, and beyond that the tunnel exit.

'Light at last,' Beckett said.

They sped out into the bright sunshine, still with the black car hugging their tail.

'We'd better get a move on,' Ros said. 'Pointless losing this lot if we turn up so late Lennox's precious launch is ruined.'

Beckett nodded. He glanced back. 'At least they've put the toys away,' he said.

'Let's hope it stays that way,' Ros said. She made a snap decision and headed for the overpass that cut across the next loop of the river. At this time of day, there would be very little traffic.

They climbed steadily, until the river was a thin blue band reeling out to either side of them. Pleasure boats as small and brightly painted as children's toys sailed along it, now hidden, now revealed by the bridge's suspension wires.

'You know they're going to have to make a move soon, don't you?' Beckett said.

Ros nodded. The question was whether Zander would be content with ruining the launch, or was determined to take the Phodex. Sure enough, as they got to the centre of the bridge, the black car accelerated. It came up on their outside, then edged in.

Ros's car rocked as the pursuers slammed into them. She fought for control of the steering as the car swerved towards the edge of the bridge.

'Come on, baby,' Ros murmured, pumping the accelerator for a last burst of speed.

The car responded. It leapt forward. Ros dragged the wheel over, simultaneously slamming on the handbrake. The car spun through ninety degrees.

Its back end whacked into the front of the black car, which pivoted round.

Ros fought for control of her car. It bucked beneath her, spun round and shuddered to a halt inches from the edge of the bridge. Before she could get her breath, Beckett nudged her.

She twisted to look back. The pursuit car had skidded round. Its shattered back end hung off the side of the bridge.

It teetered for a moment, then fell, tumbling end

over end into the river below. Ros shut her eyes. The splash came.

She looked down. The water had closed over the car as if it had never been.

'Green Machine,' Beckett said firmly, after a moment.

'Yeah,' Ros said. She pulled the car round and drove off.

'Next time, I'm driving the decoy vehicle,' Beckett said.

'Thanks,' Ros said. 'Nice to be appreciated.'

The rest of the drive passed without incident. Ed and Lennox were waiting outside The Green Machine. Ros got out of the car. There was a long swathe of paint missing across the driver's side and up onto the back of the car. She sighed, and turned her attention to work.

The restaurant was a dome constructed of tiny panes of green glass; inside, Ros could just make out a single huge tree which gave shelter from the sun, its arching branches echoing the curves of the dome.

Before she had a chance to see much more, Lennox hurried over.

'Is everything all right?' he asked

'Zander tried something, but we lost him,' Beckett said.

'We?' Ros shook her head and grinned as she shut the car door.

It was lost on Lennox, anyway. He hurried round to the car boot. 'And the Phodex is okay?'

'Yes,' Ros answered. He smiled at her and turned away to instruct the staff. 'And we're all right as well,' she said to his back. Ed shot her a what-did-you-expect look.

'Lock that in the kitchen till the chef arrives,' Lennox said to the men moving the Phodex. They went into the restaurant with the crates, and he turned back to Ros,

Ed and Beckett. 'Thank you for your help,' he said. He smiled and spread his arms expansively. 'You've played a part in making history today – you'll tell your grandchildren about this.' He looked at them expectantly.

'Mr Lennox, are you saying we can go?' Beckett asked.

'I was hoping just one of you would stay? I don't want to worry my guests unduly.' He looked them over, clearly not terribly impressed with Ed's leather jacket or Beckett's open-necked shirt. His gaze settled on Ros. 'Ros?' he said. She nodded in agreement, though in truth she'd had quite enough of the man. 'I'll see you inside, then,' he said, and left.

'While I'm doing this, you go back to New Earth Foods and dig out that file on Fricker's death,' Ros said.

'You don't trust our friend over there?' Ed asked.

'I don't trust clients who have secrets they won't reveal – especially when they also have enemies,' Ros said. Beckett nodded, and he and Ed got into her car. 'Beckett?' Ros called at the last minute.

'Yeah?'

'Don't scratch my paintwork, will you?'

She went into the restaurant, but paused in the doorway. The place was quite breath-taking. Two things caught her attention immediately. The first was the trunk of the tree, which appeared to be embedded in a chrome wall bisecting the dome. Parts of the trunk had been silvered, so that it looked as if the tree and the wall were growing together. The effect was carried on to the tree branches, which had also been wound about with wire: the whole effect was that the tree was turning into a cybernetic version of itself. The second thing that caught Ros's attention was a series of flat-screen televisions suspended from the branches of the

70

tree, so that they could be seen wherever one was sitting.

Her heels clicked on red terracotta tiles. The tabletop was a single slab of black slate, and it seemed to hang suspended in the air, though looking closer Ros could see that it was held up by thin pillars of almost invisible glass. Scattered around it were gleaming chrome planters containing shrubs, and vivid geometric displays of orchids and bromeliads so exotic they might have been crimson and sapphire origami.

How very distracting, Ros thought as she pulled out her surveillance gear. She couldn't afford to let herself be distracted – Zander certainly wouldn't.

Three men brought the Phodex into the kitchens of The Green Machine.

It looked exactly like the food it was replacing – pastries, fish, meat, vegetables and bread. Only one thing set it apart from the genuine article – uncooked, it was pale green. Pistachio colour, Lennox called it.

Publicly, Sally had agreed with him. Privately, she thought it was more the shade of pond scum.

She stared at it for a second from the security of the ventilation shaft where she had hidden herself that morning after she had slipped away from Zander.

He had just called her to say they would need plan B after all – no doubt he thought she had been waiting around for the call, and would now have difficulty carrying it out.

She hadn't bothered to tell him she had expected his stupid hired thugs to fail, and had been in position for over an hour, waiting for exactly the right opportunity.

He was so weak, so limited. He saw Phodex and saw a way to earn money. She saw Phodex and saw a way to get money without the bother of earning it. Much better. Much simpler.

71

There would never be a better chance.

She unhooked the grille covering the ventilation shaft and slipped out. She laid the titanium case she was carrying on the steel worksurface, then eased the catches open and took out the equipment she needed: a polished aluminium parabolic reflector backing a pair of spectrum-modified lighting strips, very similar in appearance to the ones used in the Phodex Propagation Chamber.

She flicked the switch on the back of the light unit, and while it was powering up, slipped on a pair of eyeshields. No point taking chances. She grinned. Lennox thought he was so clever, but the technology he'd developed to encourage hyper-growth in the Phodex was the same technology she would use to destroy him.

Just raise the frequency of the light a little and the effect on the Phodex was devastating.

Sally picked up the lightbox and held it over the first tray of Phodex. A five-second exposure should do the trick. She swept the device over the trays, being careful to make sure she got every single item.

'Mr Lennox,' said a voice just outside the kitchen door. 'All clear – no bugs, no bombs, no problems.'

Ros's voice. So the damn woman hadn't even lost her voice from that little experiment in oxygen-deprivation. Sally scowled at the Phodex as if it were somehow to blame. One more tray. Five more seconds . . . She fingered the revolver she had kept in her jacket pocket ever since she had been on Zander's payroll. She'd use it if she had to – but she'd rather not have to. It would be so messy, here. Too many questions to answer.

'I asked for champagne glasses,' Lennox said.

Done, Sally thought. She shoved the lightbox back into its case.

72

'Mr Lennox, I haven't finished yet,' Ros said. Sally hesitated. Know your enemy, she thought. She moved across to the ventilation grille, but waited there to listen. 'You paid us for a job – I'm going to stay to see it through.'

Excellent, Sally thought. She climbed into the ventilation shaft and fumbled the grille back into place. As she started to climb the access ladder, she decided that getting Lennox *and* the eminently dislikeable Ros both at once was going to be sweet indeed.

Lennox hurried up to the wall bisecting the dome of the restaurant. Ros followed him uninvited. He touched a pressure plate, and a door slid silently open. Beyond it lay the kitchens of The Green Machine. There was no pretence at melding technology with the organic here: everywhere Ros looked, she saw satined steel and gleaming chrome. And row upon row of platters of Phodex.

Lennox hurried over to one of them. He picked up a sliver of something that looked like a piece of fish made out of green modelling clay. 'Mmm,' he said. 'Smoked salmon – perfect!' Ros reached for a piece to try herself – she still didn't quite believe Phodex was all Lennox claimed. He batted her hand away. 'Patience!' he said. 'Wait for Gerard here to weave his magic . . .'

'Does that mean I'm invited to dinner?' Ros asked. She'd intended to watch from the kitchens, but it should be an interesting experience.

Lennox looked momentarily flustered. 'Oh – well, yes, I suppose.' He recovered himself. 'After all, we'll have a spare place at table – that awful girl's.'

Charmed I'm sure, Ros thought, and went to freshen up.

* * *

73

Once she was clear of The Green Machine, Sally phoned Zander.

'Phase one complete – moving to phase two,' she said, and broke the connection before he could try to tell her what to do.

She really was quite tired of being given instructions, when she had originated most of the plan herself anyway.

Ed stared over Beckett's shoulder at one of New Earth Foods' computers. A status bar showed the progress of Ros's search program.

'No trace of it,' Beckett said.

'But Ros found it yesterday,' Ed said. 'Where's it gone?'

Beckett leant back and glared at the monitor, as if their problem were its fault. 'Ros said this might happen – apparently Lennox is so paranoid about this particular file that he put extra security on it.' He played with the mouse, as if that would speed the process up. 'If it gets opened, it automatically saves itself to a different file name – a randomly generated filename – when it's closed again, and deletes the original.'

Ed shook his head and went round to boot up a second machine. 'So it's still on the local network's hard disk, but under an assumed name?'

'Yeah,' Beckett said. 'But luckily the operating system automatically records the date and time a file is created –'

'So all we have to do is search for a file that was open when Ros was attacked,' Ed said. For a second it didn't sound too bad. Then he thought about the hundreds of files that must have been in use, logging the results of minute changes in the atmosphere, temperature and growth media of the Phodex for a start, and realised they had a gargantuan job on their hands. He looked at his computer screen in despair. 'Man, this could take all night.'

'Well, you'd better get started then, hadn't you?' Beckett said.

Ros supposed she should be honoured. Lennox had given her a place right next to him. Perhaps he'd realised he might yet be in need of some protection, Ros thought. Next to her, and on the other side of the table, the guests were waiting for him to speak. According to Lennox, there were representatives of twenty-three nations, seven international bodies, eighteen major disaster relief and aid charities, and seven major religions present. If the range of dress was anything to go by – Ros saw a fair number of saris and selwar khameez, fezzes and tarbooshes among the dark business suits – he wasn't exaggerating.

Lennox stood up. He tapped his spoon against his crystal champagne flute, and everyone looked at him. 'Ladies and gentlemen – honoured guests,' he said. As he spoke there was a low hum of conversation as the simultaneous translation device that each person had been given repeated the words. 'I am deeply grateful that you have seen fit to come here today.' Ros wondered how much he had paid his image consultants and speech writers to come up with that. 'By way of introduction, may I remind you that absolutely everything you will eat here is made of Phodex.' He gestured at the dishes of fruit, nuts and candies arranged along the length of the table. 'I have devoted much of my life to developing this food, and I feel confident that in only a few years from now –' he looked significantly at the delegates from the aid charities, and Ros couldn't help but wonder exactly what price tag he would attach to any help he handed out '– in countries rich and poor, Phodex will be feeding the world.' He picked up his champagne flute. 'Let's welcome its arrival with the one thing not made from it.' Light glinted on the crystal and silver goblet as he held it up. He paused. 'Though perhaps one day . . .' There was a scattering of laughter. He waited for it to finish. 'I give you – Phodex.'

'Phodex,' chorused the assembled guests.

Waiters served the first course, and everybody ate. Against her will, Ros had to admit her truffles in champagne sauce and seafood roulade were as near to perfection as it was possible to imagine.

Ed felt as if he'd been staring at his computer screen all night, though he knew it couldn't have been more than an hour or so. Wearily, he clicked open another file, only to find that it contained temperature and growth-medium data.

Of course, if it had been the Fricker file, he wouldn't have been able to open it at all – at least not without a password, or some fairly sophisticated computer hacking.

Which gave him an idea. 'Beckett?' he called. Beckett grunted. 'That search program of Ros's – you can alter it to look for certain times, can't you?'

'Yeah,' Beckett said. 'That's how I came up with this initial list of files – they're the ones that were opened while we were at Hennessey-Brock.'

'Well, Ros said she tried to find the Fricker file just after she reconstructed the door security log –'

'So what?' Beckett asked. 'She couldn't remember exactly when that was, so it gets us no further.'

'Ros must have closed the programs down, or the Fricker file wouldn't have renamed itself,' Ed said. He knew he was on to something, but he was still trying to figure it out in his own mind as he went on slowly. 'But if we look for two programs started up within minutes of each other, we might cut our search time down.'

'Maybe,' Beckett said. He didn't sound convinced. Then again, he never did until he had the evidence in front of him. But he stopped what he was doing and reopened the search program. He thought for a couple of seconds, then tapped in some search terms.

Ten seconds later, the program had generated a list of six pairs of programs. Beckett opened them one by one.

The fourth one flashed up a warning: Enter Password.

'Now all you have to do is get into it,' Ed said. 'While you're at it, I think I'll round up some food. Want anything?'

'Just not pondweed,' Beckett said. 'Whatever Lennox says, I like to think my ham sandwich used to run around in a field, not grow in one.'

The lemon soufflé was as delightful as the rest of the meal. Ros laid down her spoon and smiled at Lennox. 'You know, that really was very good,' she said.

'Don't sound so surprised,' Lennox said. For the first time since she'd known him, he seemed completely relaxed – and much the nicer for it, Ros decided. She sipped her wine. Like the food, it was excellent.

He stood up. 'Ladies and gentlemen, having given you a taste of the extraordinary qualities of Phodex, I would now like to show you a short presentation.' He gestured to someone by the door, and the light dimmed as the glass in the dome polarised.

All around the table, crystal chinked on slate as the guests put down their glasses. The overhead screens flickered on, and the Phodex presentation began. Ros tried not to look bored, though it was the same presentation Lennox had shown the Gizmos team when he briefed them.

* * *

77

By the time Ed got back with the pizza, Beckett had hacked into the Fricker file. The executive summary was up on the screen.

'Toxins?' Ed said.

'Read all about it.' Beckett pointed to the final paragraph. 'The autopsy report showed toxins in Mr Fricker's body consistent with those generated by Phodex when it is exposed to ultraviolet light. No other cause of death could be established.'

'Man – that's what I call a product flaw.' Ed sat down, clutching the pizza box. 'How does Lennox expect to market a food that can be made poisonous?'

Beckett shot him his most cynical glance. 'By keeping the flaw a complete secret –'

Except he hadn't. 'Sally found out about this,' Ed said. He jabbed a finger at the screen. 'That's what she meant by the "Secret of Phodex".' It was clear from Beckett's expression that the same thought had occurred to both of them. 'She wouldn't,' he said.

'She might,' Beckett said. 'Come on.'

They left at a dead run.

Ros sipped her wine and watched the overhead screen. They'd just been shown the South American rainforest. That meant the shots of the Propagation Chambers were next.

She was right. And wrong.

As the picture changed, it broke up. When it reappeared words had been scrawled across it. THE PHODEX IS TOXIC – YOU ARE ALL DYING. The soundtrack cut out and was replaced with a synthesized voice that read the words out, over and over again: 'You are all dying. You are all dying.'

For a moment that was the only sound. Then someone shouted something in a language Ros didn't recognise. Others joined it. In the middle of the chaos, Lennox sat stone-still, like a robot with its power turned off.

'The Phodex is toxic,' said the voice.

A male voice cut across the hubbub. 'Will someone tell me what the hell is going on?'

'You are all dying.'

Ros leant forward. 'Mr Lennox? What does it mean?'

'The Phodex is toxic.'

'Mr Lennox,' Ros insisted. 'How can it be toxic?'

'I'll sue,' a woman said in a cut-glass British accent.

'How did they find out?' Lennox murmured. He closed his eyes. A single tear squeezed out. 'How did Zander find out?'

'You are all dying.'

'Mr Lennox, what the hell is going on?' Ros demanded. Her patience was finally at an end. 'Is this the so-called secret of Phodex?'

Lennox didn't answer, but eventually he nodded.

« Five »

Lennox could understand the Gizmos team being upset. He had been himself, when he realised what had happened. He looked at each of them in turn while they waited in the New Earth Foods laboratory for his scientists to confirm that the Phodex really had been tampered with. Ros seemed shaky but furious, Ed and Beckett simply furious.

'Sir?' said one of the scientists. He held up a beaker full of liquidised Phodex. It was bright red, rather than green. 'Strong concentrations of fulgides, I'm afraid.'

Damn, Lennox thought. He really had hoped it would turn out to be a bluff. He turned to the others. 'They weren't bluffing,' he said.

'The stuff was poisoned?' Beckett asked. Lennox wondered if there was ever a time when the man didn't scowl.

'Those two certainly have it in for you,' Ed added. He patted Ros protectively on the shoulder.

'Not poisoned,' Lennox said, wondering if there was any point at all in trying to explain it to them. They might be technological whizz-kids, but they were scientifically illiterate. Then again, most people were scientifically illiterate compared to him. 'Mutated, in a very minor way,' he added. Ros's expression said she, at least, wasn't interested in the details. Just because he felt like working out his anger on someone, Lennox continued: 'Under normal circumstances, all its by-products are harmless. Once it's been treated with ultraviolet light, one of those by-products becomes highly toxic.' Nothing he said seemed to get through to them. 'Look,' he went on, 'it only mutates under high-energy ultraviolet light, like nothing you'd find in nature.'

'Don't need to, with someone like Zander around, do you?' Beckett said.

'You think I'm a complete fool?' Lennox asked. Before Beckett could answer, he hurried on: 'We're not completely unprepared, you know – follow me.'

He led them downstairs, to the Propagation Suite. The silence, as they walked, was terrible – almost like an accusation in itself.

When he couldn't stand it any more, Lennox said, 'It was when Fricker died that we discovered the . . .' He hesitated, trying to find a way to put it that wouldn't start them on their moral crusade again. '. . . problem,' he finished at last.

'Problem,' Ros said, clearly still furious with him.

Lennox decided there was clearly no point in trying to be conciliatory, no matter what his marketing people would say. 'Phodex is perfectly safe, normally.' He searched around for an apt analogy. 'Look at electricity – it can kill you, but you still use it.'

'Yes,' Ros said, 'but we don't make it into hamburgers and sell it on the high street. What is going to happen to us?'

'We're going to take some of the antidote,' Lennox said, and was gratified to see the mortified look on all their faces. It obviously hadn't occurred to them that he might have prepared for something like this. Once was happenstance. Only a fool let it happen twice. He led them across the control area and let himself into the Propagation Suite. They followed him in. 'We keep it in the Propagation Chamber – there's a large stock, and if that's not enough it's a simple procedure to make more using raw Phodex.'

He turned to face them. They stared back stonily. Some people were simply never satisfied.

'Better hurry up and get it then,' Beckett said. 'Your guests are waiting.'

Lennox really wished he hadn't said that. The whole launch was a public relations nightmare – it was going to take very careful handling if they were to recover. He turned away, hoping they hadn't seen the look of anxiety he knew had passed across his face, and punched his ID number into the Propagation Chamber lock.

He turned to get a breathing mask on the wall. 'And we've plenty of that in here.'

He saw Ros's eyes go wide. Felt a slight tremor beneath his feet. Heat on his back. Then thunder, as the airlock door blew off its hinges. He got his arm up in time as he was thrown backwards.

A fireball gouted out from the airlock.

He slammed into the wall. Slid down.

In the corner, a small fire had started among some lab coats.

There was a second explosion, somewhere deeper in the Propagation Chamber.

Greasy smoke hung heavily in the air. He coughed. Couldn't breathe. Couldn't *breathe*.

His eyes were watering, and there was a terrible chemical stink everywhere. He blinked. The world blurred in front of him. He rubbed his eyes with the back of his hand, but that only made it worse.

Someone shouted something. Him? Maybe.

He felt a hand grab him, yank him along. He tried to crawl, but he couldn't see. Oh God, he thought. I don't want to be blinded for life.

He realised what had happened, and mentally added: what there is left of it.

The river breeze whipped at Sally's hair. Fresh, Zander had called it, when they had arrived at the boat. Damned cold, she thought. She hugged her jacket to her with one hand, watching him as he steered the boat. Her other rested lightly on the large steel canister she had brought aboard. It was the key to their future. Hers, anyway.

Smug bastard, she thought. He didn't know it, but this was his last chance.

'That explosion should have taken care of the Phodex,' he said. He didn't mention that she had planted it. 'Now they'll have to come to us for the antidote.'

Just like I said they would, Sally thought. But she stared at the buildings as they passed them, at the reflected water and sky in their mirrored sides, and said nothing.

'So it's all going to plan, then?' she asked after a moment.

'Of course,' Zander said. 'I always like to plan in detail.' Especially with me to help, Sally thought. 'We poison the guests at the launch and now we – how did you put it? Increase the pressure . . .'

Sally smiled at that. 'The money's as good as ours,' she said; but she added silently, only if you treat me right though: otherwise it's mine. All mine.

'Take the wheel,' Zander said. He stood back so she could get past him. For one moment she thought he might realise that she hadn't come unprepared, but if he did, he said nothing. Either way, he was a fool. 'I'd

84

better make our demands,' he continued. He opened a small case and took a compact broadcast antenna out of it.

Sally glanced back at him. 'Careful,' she said. 'They might try to trace it.'

'I had thought of that, Sally,' Zander said, in his usual condescending way. He wired the mobile phone to the antenna.

When she thought about it, she did remember having a conversation about this part of the plan a while ago – she'd probably pointed the danger out to him then. Of course, she'd left it to him to sort something out – she didn't want him realising just how useless he really was.

'Now, what did we decide to ask for?' Zander said. Sally hoped that was a rhetorical question. She really didn't want to think she'd got hooked up with someone so stupid he couldn't even remember that much. 'Ten million,' he said. Sally nodded. It would do, she thought. Enough to start with, anyway. 'Two million of that should see the end of your days as a lab assistant – don't you think?'

Sally felt herself go rigid with fury. It was just as well she was facing away from Zander, she thought. He couldn't possibly have mistaken the look in her eyes for anything other than what it was.

Not yet, she told herself. He still has his uses. But soon. Very soon.

Ros stared at her hands. The journey back to the Gizmos building had passed in a sickening blur.

It wasn't the fear. She was used to fear – the kind of fear she'd felt when Zander's men had chased them. That she could deal with. She relished it, even – the exhilaration of it, the adrenalin rush that lets you know you're alive, Ed had once called it.

85

But this was different. She'd never felt so helpless.

Her own body was betraying her, spreading the Phodex toxins around, letting them win. And all she could do was sit and wait, and hope that Beckett or Ed would come up with something.

Beckett had said . . . what had he said? That Zander wouldn't have gone to all that trouble just to kill a few dozen people. That he must want something. With luck, he'd swap whatever it was for the antidote. Only there was no antidote. Unless he had some antidote. He might have. Have some stashed somewhere . . .

Ros felt her thoughts spinning out of control. That wasn't good. 'Mr Lennox?' she said.

He stood by a desk near the window, while next to him Beckett set up a tracing device.

Lennox passed a hand over his eyes. 'I'm okay,' he said. He didn't look it. He was pasty white, and a muscle jumped in his jaw every now and then. 'Remember, I ate before everyone else did – the effects will be more advanced in me.'

'What happens now?' Ros asked. She had to know. She didn't want to, but she had to .

'Disorientation, loss of sensory perception –' He put out a hand to steady himself on the desk. 'Memory loss, loss of motor skills.' He looked at her. Licked his lips. Looked away. She knew what was coming, but dreaded hearing it anyway. 'And death,' he finished.

'Are you sure we shouldn't be seeking some sort of medical advice?' Beckett asked. It was useless. They'd gone over all the arguments during the drive from The Green Machine.

'No point,' Lennox said. He took a long, ragged breath. 'With the antidote gone, there's no possible source of treatment.'

'Terrific,' Ros said. Her heart was pounding. Fear, or a symptom? She didn't dare ask.

There was a blur of motion in the doorway. Ros squinted, and it resolved into Ed. Loss of sensory perception, she thought. She hadn't expected it to start so soon.

He came in, sat down and put his motorbike helmet on the table.

'What's the verdict on the chamber, Ed?' Beckett asked. 'Did any raw Phodex survive?'

Ed shook his head. 'Unfortunately, it was all boiled to a pulp.'

Ros turned to Lennox. 'You're sure there's no other way of making any antidote, Mr Lennox?'

He didn't answer, just stumbled backwards and slumped into one of the sofas. 'Can't hear,' he said. His hand groped towards his face, but he was shaking so much that it never got there. 'So dark,' he said. 'So dark.'

The phone began to ring.

'Run tape,' Beckett said.

Ros was closest to the machine. The phone rang again. She reached out to switch it on. Couldn't focus. There was supposed to be an LED by the switch. She'd built it like that. She had. But there was a strip of green light. And the tracer module. That needed turning on too, didn't it? Or would Beckett have turned it on already? She squinted at the row of switches. Okay, got to turn it on. That's what Beckett had said, wasn't it? She couldn't quite figure it out, but she reached out to do it anyway.

Her hand shook.

She was so, so cold, and her hands wouldn't stay still.

Suddenly, Ed was at her side. He touched her gently on the shoulder. 'No worries,' he whispered.

Or something. Whispered something, anyway.

He must have turned the machines on, because

Beckett picked up the phone. 'Hello, Mr Zander. Where are you calling from?'

Ros slumped back in her chair. Easier, so much easier, to let it all fall away from her.

But she mustn't. She had to concentrate. Help Beckett and Ed find Zander. Her only chance. Lennox's, too.

Beckett was doing a good job of keeping Zander talking. She heard him ask about the antidote. Then he said, 'Ten million? I don't think Mr Lennox can get that much money together just now.'

She couldn't hear Zander's reply, but Beckett exclaimed, 'You can't do that!' He listened for a moment longer. Then all the signal lights on the tracer module went out.

Beckett stared at them, visibly shaken.

'What did he say?' Ed asked.

'That he's got some of the mutated Phodex, and he's going to put it in the city's water supply if Lennox doesn't arrange an electronic funds transfer –'

'Ten million,' Ros said, repeating the one fact she was sure she had right.

'And that stuff is lethal at only four parts per billion,' Ed said. 'If it gets into the water table, he could kill everyone in the country. The world, even, if it can be taken up into the rain cycle.'

'Well, we'd better stop him, hadn't we,' Beckett said. 'Did we get it?'

Ros stared grimly at the tracer read-out until it came into focus. 'No,' she said. Beckett sighed audibly. 'Looks like he bounced it off just about every satellite up there.'

'So we got nothing,' Beckett said. His voice was full of barely suppressed fury, but Ros knew that was only his way of expressing his concern.

She tried to click the eject button on the digital tape recorder. Her hands shook so hard it took her three goes, and another couple to get hold of the tape. Even then, she almost dropped it. She held it up triumphantly. 'There's this.'

Sally watched the river unwind in front of her. They were approaching an industrial area now. The shiny office blocks had given way to squat warehouses, all yellow and red brick, and brightly enamelled exterior metalwork. This was a low-class area: the more up-market developments were a few miles upstream, nearer the centre of the city. There were fewer boats here – none of them moored, and none of them filled with sightseers.

That was good. It made things . . . simpler.

Zander patted the steel canister. 'This is a wonderful bluff,' he said. He started to put the antenna away. 'There's no way they can refuse to pay –'

'So who's bluffing?' she asked, without looking at him.

Zander appeared not to have heard her. Or if he had, he wasn't taking her seriously. Nothing different there, then.

'So where is the antidote?' he asked. 'In the canister?'

'Not exactly.' She hadn't lied to him. She'd just let him make a few unwarranted assumptions.

'What do you mean?' Zander demanded.

It was time for him to leave, Sally decided. She'd had quite enough of his demands and his assumptions and – yes – his greed. Two million pounds! It just wasn't enough.

She pulled her pistol out of her jacket pocket and whipped it round in one easy motion, while still holding the wheel with her other hand.

'What are you doing?' Zander's eyes were huge. She could almost smell the terror coming off him.

Just for a moment, she enjoyed the feel of the gun in

her hand. It was small but heavy, and the anodised steel seemed to take in the light, reflecting nothing.

'Redefining our working relationship,' she said once she had had time to savour Zander's frightened rabbit expression.

'But you can't – what are you going to do?' he said.

'Exactly what you told them,' Sally said. 'This isn't antidote – it's mutated Phodex, which I shall put into the water supply if they don't pay up.'

'But all those people – they'll die,' Zander said. 'And you were going to get a generous share –'

'Two million!' she screamed. 'Two million out of ten!'

It was nothing. *Nothing*.

She squeezed the trigger. The gun coughed in her hand. Zander spun backwards and fell against the taffrail. He clung to it. Sally fired again. For a horrible moment, she thought she might have to go and push him over. But when she fired again, his body jerked and he tumbled into the water. The undertow took him down.

Planning, Zander? Sally thought. Oh yes, I do believe in planning.

A red haze swam before Lennox's eyes. Pain throbbed at his temples, at his wrists. Something had happened. The launch. Yes. Good.

All his dreams. The launch.

But something had happened. The launch. The Phodex . . . poisoned.

Something black moved across his vision. Ed's jacket. He was waiting with Lennox. That was right. Waiting while the poison worked its way round his body.

Lennox had worked all this out before. He remembered thinking it through. How often had he worked the logic out – the Phodex launch, the poisoning. He didn't know.

But it wasn't his fault. He should try to sleep. No dreams, just sleep because it wasn't his fault. It was Zander's fault.

His eyes came wide open. Zander had poisoned the Phodex. He had to warn someone . . .

But they knew. Zander had phoned them. He was still on the phone now. Lennox could hear his voice.

How could that be?

That was right. Ros and Beckett were trying to track him down. Listen to the tape of the phone call, track him down.

So there was Zander's voice, saying: 'So how much will you pay for some antidote?'

Antidote. That was right . . . they needed antidote but the explosion had destroyed it. All of it, and his lovely Phodex too.

But Zander hadn't won. No. Because Lennox was smart. He'd saved some. He could picture it – a white light, a cold jar under his hands. A slamming door. Where was that?

In the safe. Seed material safe in the safe.

They would be safe.

He'd worked that out once before too. Forgotten it, before he could say. Mustn't do that.

He had to tell Ed. So hard though.

'Ed?' he said. He couldn't tell if he'd made a sound or not. He tried to tug Ed's sleeve. His hand wouldn't move. He concentrated on his fingers. Made them unclench. Good. Now the hand . . .

He hooked one finger into a fold in the leather. Then he had to rest.

Time to try again.

Move, he thought at his hand. Slowly, it twitched.

Ed looked round.

'Antidote,' Lennox whispered. A white balloon floated towards him, then resolved enough for him to see Ed's face. 'For the antidote – seed material.'

'What?' Ed said.

'Seed material. Last of Phodex.' He hoped he was saying it aloud.

'Where?'

Lennox wanted to explain about the light and the jar and the safe, but it was too hard. 'Glass,' he whispered. 'Glass.'

He felt Ed shake him, but it was easier just to sleep.

Beckett stood next to Ros at the audio-manipulation desk on the mezzanine floor of the Gizmos office. She was sweating, and her hands were trembling on the controls. They had listened to the tape twice without learning anything very much new.

'We'll have to try something else,' Ros said. She reached out to adjust one of the output controls, but her hand shook so much that in the end she simply laid it down on the desk.

Before he could ask what she'd intended to do, Ed shouted his name from the lower floor. Beckett hurried over to the railing.

Ed stared up at him. 'Lennox says there's something we can use to make the antidote – seed material or some such.'

Relief washed through Beckett. 'Well, get on it then,' he said.

'Yeah,' Ed said. 'But all I could get out of him was "glass".' He gestured as if drinking something.

'Glass?' Beckett murmured. Then he had it. 'He's the head of security down at New Earth Foods – go on, Ed!'

'I'm on my way,' Ed said. He got up so fast he sent his mobile chair scooting across the room. 'Hold on, Mr Lennox,' he said, and left at a dead run.

It's going to be all right, Beckett thought as he went back to Ros. No one's going to die today.

She was slumped over the equipment. He touched her gently on the shoulder. She sat up. He wanted to tell her to get some rest, that he would deal with everything – but he knew she would hate that. Her expression said that she was going to fight till the end. A muscle under her eye began to jump.

He thought about telling her about the seed material, but decided against it: best not to raise her hopes.

'You sure you're up to this?' Beckett asked. At that moment, if he could have got his hands on Zander and Sally he would have ... well, best not to think of what he would have done. Ros's only chance was for them all to stay focused.

'I've got to be,' she said. She folded her arms and tucked her hands under her armpits. Beckett knew why that was – she didn't want to let him see her shake. Or herself. 'Take out the speech and bring up the ambient sound.' Beckett fiddled with the controls. He'd seen her do this often enough. He only wished he'd taken more notice himself. 'We used to do this all the time in college – testing each other.' She looked at him. Her eyes were glassy. 'It was just a game then ...'

'When this is all over you can test me,' Beckett said. 'Got to share those skills around, you know.' He smiled. Ros didn't smile back. 'You ready for this?' he asked when he'd done his best with the audio controls.

Ros nodded. She closed her eyes. Her head lolled to one side. For one terrible moment Beckett thought she had lost consciousness. Then he realised she was simply trying to concentrate. He started the tape.

Without the voices, the background noise was much clearer – water, for sure. An engine. That was about as good as Beckett could do.

'We're on a boat,' Ros said dreamily. 'A small one, probably a pleasure boat. Small engine. Could be solar-powered. On open water – there's not much backwash. No waves, either, so it's a river not the sea. Can you hear that?'

'Just about,' Beckett said, though he could barely make out what she meant.

The sounds of splashing grew much louder. 'We're going under a bridge,' Ros said. 'Listen to the backwash now.'

It was clear enough. Beckett moved across to the map tank on the next desk. 'Listen, Ros,' he said as gently as he could, 'we're going to have to narrow it down just a bit more.'

Ros swallowed. She nodded. The sound of a plane roared out of the speakers. 'That should help,' she said. 'It sounds like it's coming in to land.'

Beckett flicked the switch on the tank, and a three-dimensional hologram of the city shimmered into existence. Quickly, he used the map's search facilities to find waterways with bridges that were also near airports. 'This is hopeless,' he said. 'According to this search, there are nearly a dozen airports near rivers or canals, if you count private airfields.'

'Let me listen to it again,' Ros said.

Beckett leant over and rewound the tape for her. She clearly wasn't capable of doing it herself. Her skin was waxy, and sheened with sweat, yet her lips looked dry and cracked.

He pressed play. Again, the aircraft noise roared out. 'That sounds a bit odd, doesn't it?' he asked, feeling quite proud of himself for picking up the strangeness. 'Too powerful, maybe?'

'Let me hear it again,' Ros said. Beckett rewound the tape and pressed 'play'. When she'd finished listening to it, Ros said, 'That's no jet – it's a VTOL.'

'Vertical take-off and landing craft?' Beckett said. 'But there's only one place near the city that regularly handles those . . .'

'Just our luck, eh, Beckett?' Ros said.

Beckett scrolled the map to show the area around the VTOL field. It looked as if their luck had run out. The whole area was laced with the blue of rivers and canals, and there were any number of bridges.

Ros glanced over. 'I'll cross-reference the other sounds,' she said. He saw her knuckles go white on the audio station's controls. 'I can do this,' she muttered.

'In time?' Beckett asked, then wished he hadn't. Hope was the only thing she had to hold on to, however misplaced it was.

'I have to,' she said. 'Get on the road – head for that area and I'll give you more directions when I can.'

Beckett nodded. He headed for the stairs. Behind him, he could hear the rasp of Ros's breathing. He turned. 'What about you?' he asked.

'Just stop them poisoning any more people,' she said.

Beckett stared at her for a long moment. If she died, here, alone ... If that happens, Zander, Beckett thought, you'd better start running; but wherever you go, I *will* find you.

Ed followed Glass up the stairs of New Earth Foods to Lennox's private office.

'This way,' Glass said. 'Mr Lennox only recently had the safe installed – he was scared of an attack, you see.'

'What's the locking system?' Ed said. He wasn't particularly interested in making polite conversation – not with Ros, Lennox and all his guests in direct danger, and the whole country under threat – but that subtlety seemed to have escaped Glass. 'Combination?' That could be tricky, depending on the number of digits involved, and the sensitivity of the system – he'd probably have to break into it manually; luckily, he had a miniaturised microphone that would help him hear the tumblers fall and –

'No,' Glass said. He led Ed into Lennox's office. The safe was a ball of silvery metal, cradled on a glass stand.

'Computer-coded?' Ed asked. In a way, that was better. He had a piece of software on the palmtop computer he always carried that could probably break it in time, no problem.

'No,' Glass said.

'Well, what is it then?' Ed snapped, thoroughly fed up with Glass's game-playing.

'It's a timelock.' Glass almost sounded smug. 'It's not programmed to open till nine o'clock.'

Ed looked at his watch. 'I can't wait that long,' he said. The file had said that Fricker had died three hours after the onset of his first symptoms. By that reckoning, Ros had something under an hour left. He dropped to his knees and flipped open his toolkit, looking for anything that might help.

'Not nine tonight,' Glass said. 'Nine on Monday morning – you won't get in there this side of the weekend.'

Yes I will, Ed thought. He had to. It was that simple.

« Six »

Ed prodded at the delicate tracery of circuits that made up the control mechanism of the safe's timelock. Staring at it through the powerful magnification of his micro-binoculars was almost like looking at a city from a helicopter, with the circuits replacing roads, and the chips buildings.

He touched one of the output pins with the tip of his probe. He was attempting to analyse the signal the circuit sent to tell the lock to open, so that he could replicate it. The monitoring program in his palmtop computer beeped. He tried the next pin. The beep rose to a continuous screech.

He flipped the micro-bins up onto his forehead, blinked until his eyes adjusted to the larger world, then glanced at the screen. Not good. Three lines of text told him that the safety interlocks had registered two attempts to breach security. One more and the safe would go into lockdown mode: the door would physically weld itself shut.

Obviously he needed to think of a different approach.

He handed Glass the palmtop and stood up, glad of the opportunity to stretch his legs. He walked round the safe. Maybe if brains wouldn't work, brute force would?

He slapped the top of the safe. 'I suppose this is three-inch-thick titanium?' he asked.

'Oh yes,' Glass said. 'Actually, it's reinforced with ortho-carbon mesh –'

'So blowing a hole in it isn't a possibility,' Ed said, running his hand over it. It really was a very nice piece of work.

'Mr Lennox said it would take an atom bomb to get into it,' Glass said, clutching the gear Ed had given him as if he thought it might explode.

'Yeah, well I don't think I can get hold of one of those in time,' Ed said.

By his reckoning, Ros had maybe forty-five minutes left.

The time was just slipping by, and he wasn't any closer to a solution.

And then he was.

He came round to the front of the safe again. 'If this thing won't open till Monday,' he said, 'we'll just have to persuade it that it is Monday.'

He pulled the micro-bins down over his eyes again. This time, he connected his equipment to one of the input pins. The display on the palmtop showed that all security had been by-passed. That was easy, Ed thought uneasily. But the safe's LCD display showing the date and time flickered and changed to 08:59, Monday, and he dismissed his worries.

'You should be able to open the safe now,' Ed said.

There were a few muffled thumps. 'It won't open,' Glass said.

Ed took the probe away from the input pin. The LCD reverted to the proper date. 'What?' he said.

'Oh,' Glass said, 'I didn't really think you'd be able to fool it – it takes a direct feed off the Time Signal.'

So all I did was change the display – not the time set in the actual clock, Ed thought. He was close to despair when the implications of what Glass had said sunk in. 'Well, you could have told me that before,' he snapped.

Beckett was beginning to worry. He'd been driving for twenty minutes, and he had passed the VTOL field a while ago, but he hadn't heard from Ros for what seemed like an eternity. He adjusted his headset, then said into the mike, 'Ros?'

No reply.

Beckett stared at the map on the computer screen set into his dashboard. It was a two-dimensional representation of the one in the map tank at Gizmos. Okay, he thought. Stay calm. She's probably okay – just concentrating. The only thing I can do to help her now is to find Zander and Sally.

He located his position on the map. There were several rivers in the area. Only a couple of bridges though. Now, if he could just –

'Beckett?' Ros said. Her voice sounded faint, slurred.

Relief washed through him. 'I've just come off the elevated roadway two miles west of the VTOL field,' he said, struggling to sound calm. If Ros thought he'd been worried, she'd get more stressed than she must already be, and that could only be bad.

'There should be a mag-lev rail somewhere to the north of you,' Ros said.

'I'm there,' Beckett said.

'Turn right under it.' The sound of Ros's breathing – harsh, laboured – came over the radio.

Beckett hung a right. Ahead of him there was the embankment of the river. He pulled over to the side of the road while he decided what to do next. On the opposite shore, a white and silver tower speared into the sky, flanked on either side by smaller buildings. On his side of the river, the road climbed up to become a bridge. The mag-lev rail was slung underneath it. Even as Beckett watched, the silver bullet of a City Special rocketed along it, taking passengers from the VTOL field into the centre of the city. Well, he didn't want to go that way, that was for sure, he thought. The other option was the road that flanked the river.

'I've found the river,' Beckett said. He didn't add that he couldn't be sure it was the right one. 'Which way were they going – could you tell?'

'Up,' Ros said. The word was hardly more than a breath. 'Upstream.'

'Right,' Beckett said. He set off again. If they were still on the boat, he supposed he might spot them, but otherwise they could be anywhere.

'Beckett?' Ros said. 'Beckett – I know where they're heading.' For a long moment, the only sound was the sharp rasp of her breathing. Beckett resisted the impulse to tell her to go on. 'Pumping station,' she said after a long while. 'Treatment centre. North. Five.' Minutes? Beckett wondered. Miles? 'Stop them, Beckett . . . stop them.'

There was a muted bang. A slithering sound. A duller thump.

'Ros!' Beckett shouted. His imagination filled in the details: Ros falling forward, and then off her chair.

You'll pay for this, Zander, Beckett thought. I don't care what it takes – you will pay.

Sally took the mutated Phodex out of its canister. There wasn't much light in the pumping station – it wasn't necessary in an automated facility. Still, she couldn't help but admire the algae's wonderful green colour.

She was going to do magic. She was going to turn

that green into the colour of money. And it was all going to be hers.

She had already switched off the water supply to the treatment unit she had selected. Now she reached up and pulled the fluoride canister off it. As she touched the metal, she felt the throb of the pumping machinery thrill through her hand.

Carefully, she poured the Phodex from its phial into the fluoride holder in the treatment unit.

Next, she picked up the timeswitch she had brought with her. Such a simple thing, she thought, looking at it – just a switch attached to a clock. They'd pay up, or at the appointed time – the time she would set, no one else – the switch would turn the treatment unit back on and Phodex full of fulgide toxins would flood into the water. No amount of filtration or additives would remove it.

Of course, it wouldn't come to that. She'd fax directions telling them where to find the Phodex in plenty of time. Assuming they paid up. And they were nice to her. That Ros woman had been so unpleasant, she really did need to be taught a lesson – one like Lennox had been given would do very nicely.

Before she could attach the timeswitch to the treatment unit, she heard a noise.

It was a minor setback, nothing more. It was just as well she'd come prepared to deal with emergencies.

Ros hurt.

Something was digging into her face. Headset, she thought. Or the mesh of the floor. There was a bright light shining in her eyes, but she couldn't find the energy to close them. Her head felt as though it had been pumped full of molten lead.

But it was all right. She didn't have to do anything. Just lie there. Let the pain wash over her.

I'm dying, she thought.

It didn't seem to matter.

Ed made a minute adjustment to the synthesiser he was using. On the LCD screen of his palmtop, two signal frequency patterns were superimposed on each other. The original was red; Ed's copy, green. As he made the adjustment, the green one became a closer match for the red.

'What are you doing?' Glass asked from behind him.

Ed's hand jerked. Now the green pattern was very different from the red one.

'Learning to travel in time,' he said. He really wished that Glass would go away. Every few minutes, the man asked some inane question, and Ed could have done without the distraction. Painstakingly, he readjusted his signal.

'What?' Glass asked.

It was probably going to be easier to explain once and for all, Ed decided. 'I've located the incoming time signal,' he said. That had been the easy part. All New Earth Foods' clocks used it. He'd simply found a junction box so far away from the safe's inputs that it had no defence against him. 'If I can reproduce the exact frequency, then I can regulate the clock.'

'To make it go quicker,' Glass said.

Bright boy, Ed thought. 'That's the general idea,' he said, and smiled.

Just then the palmtop bleeped, and a message appeared across the frequency display:

Match achieved: 99.95 accuracy.

Proceed? Yes/No.

'That's as good as it's going to get,' Ed said. He clicked the 'yes' button.

Now his smile was genuine.

* * *

Beckett's car screeched to a halt. He leaped out and looked around. The jutting silver cylinder of the pumping station dominated this section of the river bank. It was fully automated. One quick phone call while he was on his way had established that. A motor launch was tied up at a jetty nearby. Its prow and stern were covered in black solar-energy collectors.

It still might not be Zander's, Beckett thought – but he'd better be ready in case it was.

He hurried over to the entrance of the pumping station. The lock had clearly been gimmicked, and the door slid silently open at his touch. He was sure, now, that Zander was already there.

He went inside, and found himself peering into darkness that was filled with the humming of a hundred, a thousand pumps. He was standing on one of many walkways that ran around the perimeter of the cylinder in ranked tiers. They were supported by thick vertical pipes, from which floodlamps were suspended: but the light they gave illuminated little, for the pipes and walkways were made of blue anodised steel.

Beckett touched one of the pipes. It was freezing cold, and it thrummed slightly beneath his hand.

A neat piece of design, Beckett thought: the pipes not only supported the walkways, they also carried the water round the station.

He looked down, and immediately regretted it. The cylinder plunged a couple of hundred metres down, so that the lamps at the bottom were pinpricks of light in the darkness. His hand gripped reflexively at the railing. He forced himself to look up, and found that just as dizzying. A tiny dot of brightness in the distance must be skylight in the top of the station, he decided.

Metal clinked on metal.

Beckett's head jerked round. The sound had come from somewhere above him.

Three tiers above him, shadows moved in the darkness, black on midnight blue. It might have been one person, or many. With so many light sources it was impossible to tell.

He waited, but the sound did not come again. The shadows stopped moving, became one with the other shadows on the curved cylinder wall.

Beckett made his way round the gallery. His feet rang on the perforated steel walkway, making any attempt at silence useless.

He came to a ladder. It led up. And down, through a hole in the walkway. It would be so easy to slip here.

To pinwheel down, past walkway after walkway, speed tearing the breath from his lungs, arms flailing to grasp at anything that might stop him hurtling downward to destruction, fingers perhaps brushing metal as they passed but never closing . . .

The world seemed to spin in front of him. He closed his eyes, forced himself to think of Ros, dying. Ros, whose last words to him had been to save others.

He grasped one of the rungs, swung his leg over the void and stepped onto the ladder. The treads were, at least, heavily textured.

He began to climb.

It was easy at first, but gradually the muscles in his thighs began to ache. His hands hurt from the metal treads, and he could not quite forget the drop that waited for him if he made a mistake.

Thirty rungs. Forty. The first walkway above him. The second. A fall from even that height would kill him, but the cylinder was ten or twenty times deeper.

Don't look down, Ed had said. Don't look anywhere.

Beckett didn't mean to, but to think it was to do it. He glanced down, and saw an infinity of receding walkways, each one barely visible through the ladder access above it.

Sweat glazed his palms. His hands slipped. His foot –

He grabbed at the rung. Made it. Wrapped his arm around it and leaned against the ladder with the breath sobbing out of him.

The only way to end it was to climb.

Another ten rungs. Fifteen.

He climbed through the final walkway, then stepped off the ladder. There was no strength in his legs. His arms trembled. He leaned against the railing for support, and tried to ignore the abyss that spread itself below him.

Something cold and hard laid itself against his neck, just behind his ear.

He froze. 'Don't do anything rash, Mr Zander,' he said.

'It isn't Zander you have to worry about,' said Sally's voice. Beckett started to turn. 'Hands behind your back,' she snapped.

'Where is Zander?' Beckett said, as he did as he was told. His only hope was to keep her talking. With luck he'd get a break somewhere down the line.

'Feeding the fishes,' Sally said. He felt her wrap something round his wrists. 'Don't struggle,' she warned, yanking on the bindings hard enough to make him flinch. 'This is mono-molecular fibre wrapped in a high-density polymer. You'll be fine if you keep still. Struggle, and the fibre will slice through the polymer like a wire through cheese. Then it'll do the same to your wrists.' She sounded quite happy with the idea. She grabbed his headset. 'You won't be needing this.'

She threw it over the railing, and it fell into the abyss, now catching the light, now disappearing into shadow, until finally it was gone.

'Do you know how much those things cost?' Beckett asked, trying to keep his tone light. Rule one – talk to your captor, make them see you as human.

'Don't patronise me,' Sally said. She shoved Beckett viciously between the shoulder blades. 'Move.'

Beckett stumbled forward.

The time display on the safe lock flickered and changed: 08:57, 08:58, 08:59.

09:00.

There was a loud click and a servo-motor hummed briefly.

'Yes!' Ed shouted. He withdrew his probe and flipped up his micro-binoculars. 'We've done it!' He turned to Mr Glass, who smiled as if he'd done most of the work. 'Better tell your white-coat boys to stand by to whip up a batch of antidote,' he said.

He opened the safe door. Inside it, there was a second door.

'Mr Lennox is very security-conscious,' Glass said.

Just as well one of you was, Ed thought. He pulled at the handle on the inner door, but it wouldn't budge. That was when he noticed a small panel set into the centre of the door. He flipped it open.

An LCD screen with a small keyboard set flush to the surface of the door confronted him.

He looked more closely at the screen. 'Password?' it said.

'Password? I don't believe it,' Ed said. The unfairness of it, after he had tried so hard, boiled through him. He slammed his hand into the side of the safe, and turned to Glass. 'Do you know what it is?' he demanded.

Glass stared at him blankly. 'No,' he said, in his slow way. 'Mr Lennox wouldn't tell me.'

'Does he keep a note of it?' It was all Ed could do to

stop himself shaking Glass. 'Think man – is it the name of his wife? His kid?' Still Glass stared at him. 'His dog?'

'I don't *know*,' Glass said, finally sounding upset. He licked his lips. 'But he does forget things – he keeps an organiser. It's always in his jacket pocket.'

And that, of course, was back at Gizmos. Ed glanced at his watch. There wasn't time to go and get it. Not even on the bike. Not even if he broke all the speed limits and ran through every red light he came to.

It's up to you now Ros, he thought. He flicked the switch on his radio mike. 'Ros?' he said. 'Ros?'

There was no answer.

Beckett walked into the gloom. Ahead of him, he could just make out a bank of equipment. Control panels glowed neon under tiers of chemical-input tanks.

He could hear Sally's footsteps behind him, feel her breath on the back of his neck. Or maybe he imagined it. It didn't matter. He didn't dare stop or look round. All he could do was keep walking.

As he got closer Beckett saw an insulated flask sitting on the floor. It was open, and there was a large test-tube next to it. It was scummy green, and for a moment hope surged through him. Maybe it was full. Maybe she hadn't done anything stupid yet. Anything irreversible.

Then he saw the stopper next to it, and realised that it was empty. Next to it on the floor there was a small pile of electronic gear. A remote control? No. There was an LCD display in the pile, and it was showing the time.

Okay, he thought. If she's got it on a time delay, maybe I can still talk her out of this.

'Why are you doing this?' he asked. 'You don't want to kill all those people –'

'No I don't,' Sally said. 'But I do want my money – and I'll do what I must to get it.' She darted round in front of him. Light gleamed on her gun. It was snub-nosed, a neat little RFG repeater. Eight bullets, Beckett remembered from his reading. Not six – that could be important. But with Zander dead, she might already have fired it. He wondered if she'd thought to reload it. It wasn't something he cared to ask her. She jabbed the gun at him. He stopped walking. 'Why isn't Lennox taking me seriously?' she demanded.

'The last time I saw Lennox he was unconscious,' Beckett said. Sally thrust the gun at him again. She was holding it in both hands, and she didn't look comfortable with it. 'He could be dead by now,' Beckett finished. So could Ros, but he wasn't going to tell Sally that: it would give her too much leverage over him.

'You could have got the money,' Sally said. Her pale skin was ghostly in the bluish light. 'You still could.' She stepped a little closer to him. A smile played across her mouth. 'I'm sure there are many who'd pay for the privilege of drinking pure water.' She sounded quite excited by the idea.

It isn't the money, Beckett thought. She thinks it is, but it's the feeling of power she enjoys. He wondered if there could be any reasoning with her at all. 'How can I get you anything when I'm tied up like this?' he said.

Sally stepped away from him. 'You're just like Lennox – you aren't taking me seriously either.' She went over to the nearest bank of equipment. Now Beckett realised that the lid had been taken off one of the chemical additive flasks. A tube led from it to a second flask inside the main tank. And in that second flask there was an all too familiar green liquid.

'Four parts per billion,' Sally said. 'At that rate, this one flask of Phodex is enough to contaminate the whole of the city's water supply.' She bit her lip, obviously delighted with herself. How could anyone so attractive be so twisted, Beckett wondered. 'Shall I tell you how I'm going to do it?' she asked.

'I'm sure you won't be happy till you have,' Beckett said. Got to keep her talking, he thought. The longer he strung her along, the greater the chance he'd find something he could use against her.

'When this switch is turned on, water enters the chamber here, and mixes with the mutated Phodex,' Sally said. She traced its route with her finger. Beckett took the opportunity to look around. There had to be something he could use. Anything. 'When the water level reaches this outflow, the Phodex will enter the main water supply for the city.'

Something glinted on the wall to Beckett's right. He forced himself not to look at it directly, but only with his peripheral vision. Alarm bell, maybe? It couldn't be anything much else.

'So,' he said. 'You going to let me go so I can get your money, or what?'

'Do you think I'm that stupid?' Sally said. 'I was going to put it on a timeswitch – give you time to get the money to me – but you ruined that plan, Mr Clever Clever Beckett.' Her finger hovered over the 'start' button. 'No,' she said. 'There's nothing else for it – I'll just have to make what I can out of selling the anti-dote.'

Her finger jabbed at the button.

Water gushed into the tank.

Someone, somewhere was saying Ros's name.

That wasn't right. She was dead. They couldn't bother her now.

But they were. He was. She concentrated. It was Ed's voice, coming over her headset.

'Talk to me, Ros,' Ed said.

She wanted to tell him to go away. So much easier to lie here, even with the mesh biting into her cheek, and the pain in her arms and legs and head. But she knew he wouldn't. Not Ed. Persis ... persis ... persomething, that was Ed.

She managed to get her hand to move, to push her mike closer to her mouth. 'Ed,' she said.

He said something back to her. She couldn't hear it properly. It kept turning to garble, like a signal degraded by white noise.

Got to concentrate, she thought. People dying. Someone was, anyway.

'Organiser,' Ed said. She heard that one word, then more garble. 'Lennox.' Got that, she thought. Just be quiet now, Ed. Let me sleep. But Ed kept on making words at her. 'Pocket,' he said.

'Organiser,' Ros said, hoping that would satisfy him. 'Lennox. Pocket.'

'Good!' Ed said. 'Get it.' Garble garble garble in her ear.

He must think he was making sense, Ros thought. 'What?' she said. It was so hard to get her tongue round the word, to force herself to breathe sound into it.

'Get it,' Ed said.

'Ed, I can't.' She didn't even know if the words would sound right.

The world was a blur of blue and yellow before her eyes. It hurt her eyes. But Ed was saying something to her. Had said something to her. She thought about it. What had he said? It was important. Something he'd said was, she was sure.

Antidote. That was it. Get the organiser, get the antidote.

Not die.

Not die!

110

But it was so hard. Her whole body felt like it was made of lead. She commanded her arms and legs to move. Nothing happened.

One at a time, then.

Pain seared through her limbs, jolted into her spine and across her shoulders. Ignore it, she thought. It's only pain. Pain is good. Alive if you can feel pain.

She managed to get up onto all fours, then grabbed her desk and used it to lever herself upright.

A wave of nausea washed over her. Pain knotted her stomach. The room shimmered in front of her. She swayed and would have fallen over, but managed to grab the desk again.

She took one step in the direction of the stairs. Another. Now there was nothing to hold on to.

I can do this, she thought. She took a deep breath. It wheezed in her chest.

She tried to take another pace, and fell towards the rail of the mezzanine. She stared down into a blur of colours that should have been the downstairs office. The mesh of the rail bit into her fingers. She squinted hard. Shapes formed out of the fog.

Lennox, sprawled across the sofa. He was maybe ten metres away, across and down.

It might as well have been as many light-years.

Ed turned to Glass. He was breathing as hard as if he had done a parachute jump, run five miles and then abseiled down a cliff face.

Come to think of it, he'd rather have done that than bully Ros the way he had.

'Ed,' she said. 'I can't do this, it's too far and please just let me go to sleep.' The words slurred into each other.

'You mustn't, Ros,' he said. 'Just take it one step at a time. Slow as you like, but just do it.'

111

'I'll try, Ed,' Ros said. Her voice sounded faint and sleepy.

Ed turned to Glass. 'She can do this,' he said firmly. He only wished he was as certain as he sounded.

One step at a time, Ros thought.

She hung on to the banister rail, and let her feet slide down each step. Every time she landed, pain jolted through her.

That was okay though. Mustn't go to sleep.

She had been halfway down the stairs when she finally worked out what Ed meant. He might be able to make some antidote.

That was important. That was worth fighting for.

She ran out of banister rail, and tried to take a step forward without it.

The world twisted in front of her. She fell.

Nobody's saying I have to make it on my two feet, she thought, and began to crawl foward. Every movement sent pain like gouts of fire screaming through her.

And then something blue and solid loomed out of the fog her world had become.

The sofa. Lennox. Why was that important?

Ed had told her to. 'Ed?' she whispered. 'Lennox.'

He said something. An important word. Right. Get the organiser.

She knew where it would be. Ed had told her, but that had been half a lifetime ago, and she couldn't remember. She had to. He'd only garble at her again if she asked him.

Jacket. The word floated into her mind.

She fumbled at Lennox. Hair. That soft stuff she could feel was hair. This was skin.

And this was his jacket.

She fumbled inside it. Found something hard and flat. Dragged it out.

'I've got it,' she said. Or thought she said. She tried to open the organiser. Her fingers wouldn't do what she told them. It was as if they belonged to someone else, someone who had big fat clumsy fingers like sausages. 'Can't open it.'

Ed said something to her. It was important. She concentrated as hard as she could. '– time,' he said.

Yes, time. Nearly no time left.

She jabbed at the organiser again, and this time it sprang open. ''Min,' she muttered.

Buttons. Lots of buttons.

Ed was talking again. This time she listened really hard. 'Memo,' he said.

She knew about buttons. She could do buttons. But which one would be memo? She had an organiser just like this one. Very popular model. She'd known once, like she knew how to breathe.

The organiser floated in and out of focus.

Don't think about it, just do it. She ran her fingers over the top row of buttons.

Then pressed.

If she was wrong, she was never going to be able to get back to the main screen to try again.

'Got it,' she said. She screwed up her eyes. 'Something written here.' She moved the screen, trying to get a better look at it. 'Can't read it though.'

'Can,' Ed said, and lots of other stuff that was too difficult to listen to.

'Think it begins with an M,' Ros said. 'Mmmm . . .' It was just too hard. She couldn't do it any more, no matter what Ed said. 'Ros go sleep now,' she said.

Ed took a deep breath. Ros had been doing so well, but now she had gone quiet. He stared around at the brightly lit New Earth Foods office.

Sunshine poured in the windows.

113

How could it be such a beautiful day, when one of his closest friends was about to die – he wouldn't countenance the idea that she might already be dead – and there was nothing he could do to save her?

I should have taken the bike, he thought. I'd have found a fast enough route. Anything but sitting here uselessly like this.

The only thing he could do was talk to her. 'Ros,' he said. 'Listen to me, Ros – just look at it again, okay?' A soft moan came out of his earpiece. Thank God, he thought. She was still alive. That was something. 'In your own time, Ros,' he said. 'Do it for me, please Ros.'

'Try,' she whispered. There was a long pause. Ed almost thought he'd lost her again. 'Mmm,' she said. 'Mad? Could be Mandy?'

'Has he got a wife or daughter called Mandy?' Ed asked Glass. He was terrified to try what might be an incorrect password, in case the safe went into lock-down.

Glass shook his head.

'Man?' Ros said. 'Something like that . . .'

'Man,' Ed repeated, trying the sound of it out. 'Man, Mandy, mandible, mantra . . .' And then he had it. 'Manna! Manna from heaven. That has to be it.'

He sprinted over to the safe. With the screen facing him, he was suddenly not so sure. But there was no help for that. Carefully, he typed in the word: *Manna*.

There was a dull click. The inner door sprang open. Ed opened it the rest of the way. There, bathed in bluish radiance, was the jar of Phodex seed material.

Ed picked it up almost reverently. He was torn between the need for speed and the absolute necessity of keeping it safe. He cradled it in his arms as Glass led him down to the laboratories.

Half a dozen white-coated scientists were waiting

for him, their equipment already set up so they could get straight to work.

Ed laid the jar down in front of the leader. 'All right, my friend,' he said to her. 'Do your thing.'

'These deaths,' Sally said. 'They'll be your responsibility as well. The streets will be full of corpses.' Behind her, the water rose in the tank. It was already halfway to the top, its green colour leaving no room for doubt.

'All right,' Beckett said quietly. He could feel the SID in his back pocket. If he could get it without her noticing, he might still be in with a chance. 'You've made your point. Turn the water off.'

Sally's face contorted into a mask of rage and hate. 'I want money!' she screamed. Then suddenly the anger was gone. She smiled at Beckett, and for the first time he realised that she was actually quite mad. 'And,' she said girlishly, 'you can help me get it.'

His fingers groped at the SID. Almost there. A centimetre more. As long as she didn't notice what he was doing. As long as the coating on his bindings didn't wear through ... he'd seen what mono-molecular fibre could do. It wasn't pleasant.

He swallowed. 'Look, I can get the money for you, okay?' She nodded. The look in her eyes was pure craziness. 'But I can't get it here, can I? You'll have to take me back to the office –' That was almost too much. 'You'll have me as a hostage. No one will try anything ...'

'Nice try,' Sally said. 'But it isn't going to work. Maybe I don't care, did you ever think of that? Maybe I just don't care how I get the money, just as long as I do.'

The SID slipped into Beckett's hands.

'Even if you can get more money doing it this way?' he asked. That seemed to be the key. She stared at him like a cobra fascinated by a mongoose. 'I can, you know,' he said.

One chance.

He pushed the button on the SID. The alarm squealed.

Sally jerked round. Beckett aimed a drop-kick at her. He caught her arm, but the gun went off.

Three shots went wild into the darkness.

Sally brought the gun round to bear on him again. 'Like I said, nice try,' she said. 'I think I've had enough of you, Mr Beckett.' She jerked her head towards the railing. 'Over there.'

Light glinted on the gun barrel. How many shots, Beckett thought desperately. If it were fully loaded ... she might have used more than one bullet on Zander, but the damn gun carried eight rounds.

He backed off slowly. She followed him.

'You'll land so hard they'll have to identify you from a DNA analysis,' Sally said. Something moved behind her.

Light on water.

'Sally!' Beckett screamed. 'Behind you!'

'You won't get me that –' she said.

Her final words were lost in the thunder as a wave of water and glass crashed down on her. She opened her mouth, but Beckett couldn't hear her scream.

He launched himself backwards, and managed to roll towards the bank of equipment.

Sally's feet slipped from under her. She rolled towards the edge, appearing and disappearing in the roiling mass of water.

Then suddenly it was over. Water still flowed towards the walkway edge, but in a steady stream rather than a boiling tidal wave.

Beckett looked around. The shots had taken out the sides of one of the reservoirs, leaving only a jagged edge of glass around its rim.

Luck had been with him, though. It wasn't the one containing the Phodex. He glanced at that tank. The Phodex was within a centimeter of the outflow valve.

He was on his way to it when Sally's voice screamed, 'Help me!'

He spun round. Sally's face peered up at him out of the darkness. Her eyes were huge and terrified. Her hands were clenched desperately around the top rail of the walkway. The water pouring over the side battered at her.

He hesitated. Glanced back.

The Phodex rose inexorably towards the valve.

'Hold on,' he shouted.

He raced towards the tank, then turned and groped for the off-switch. He couldn't look at it and press it at the same time. Third one down. The only round one. His fingers traced the shapes of the button. Counted them. Pressed.

The equipment bleeped. He turned. The Phodex had stopped rising within a millimetre or two of the out-flow.

Sally screamed. Beckett turned. She was nowhere to be seen . The sound of her voice reverberated around the cylinder, then died away.

Moments later, there was a thunderous crash.

Beckett hurried across and looked down. Far below, there was a seething mass of water that was slowly filling the station. In it floated a small coloured object that had to be Sally.

As he watched, the object turned around in the water, tumbled over and disappeared from sight.

Ed raced through the Gizmos building, leading two of the New Earth Foods scientists.

He slammed open the door to the office where they had been working. Lennox was sprawled over the sofa,

117

more or less where he had been when Ed left him. His skin was creamy, and there was a faint blue blush around his mouth.

And Ros . . .

At first he couldn't see her. Then he spotted her. She was lying on the floor behind the sofa. He rushed over to her.

She didn't seem to be breathing. He laid two fingers against her neck. There was the faintest flutter of a pulse.

He looked up at the scientist. 'She's still alive,' he said.

The scientist already had the hypodermic out. She pushed the plunger, and a droplet of greenish fluid shone briefly in the air.

She turned to Ed. 'Your friend will be fine,' she said. 'So will Mr Lennox, and his guests.'

She went to Lennox and gave him his injection. Then she did the same for Ros.

Ed stroked Ros's back gently.

'So tired,' she murmured.

'It's okay,' he said. 'You sleep now, Ros. Everything's going to be fine.'

« Seven »

Behind its defensive railings, the Millennium Metals building loomed out of the darkness of a moonless sky.

Joseph Da Silva strolled up to it as if he had every right, despite the lateness of the hour. A guard approached from the other side and Da Silva recognised him as Wallace. He stopped in front of the gates, looked round once – the weak man's instinct, Da Silva thought, not to trust his own planning – and wiped his cardkey through the lock.

The gates hummed open on their servo-motors. Da Silva slipped inside and they shut behind him. He started to follow Wallace across the courtyard.

'The R6 is in the sound-proof vault?' he asked.

Wallace nodded. 'Just like I told you,' he said, gesturing at a small high-security door set into the wall near the main entrance. 'It's through there.'

Da Silva pulled a lead-weighted cosh out of his pocket and brought it crashing down on the back of Wallace's head. The man dropped to the floor.

Da Silva took the cardkey out of Wallace's hand. Then he stepped over the body and hurried towards the vault door.

He attached an MDX bomb to the lock area, then moved back. Setting up the sound suppressor took only a few moments. Above his head, a security monitor winked in the floodlights. Nothing to worry about. It was already taken care of.

He pointed the remote control at the bomb, and pressed the trigger.

Black smoke billowed silently outwards. Vibration thrummed through the soles of Da Silva's feet. It was the single weak link in the chain of his planning – the one thing he hadn't been able to control.

Speed was his best defence. He tore towards the soundproof chamber. It was on the far side of the vault. He hurried past metal shelves holding stacks of gold ingots, piles of platinum, all stamped with the Millennium Metals logo.

So tempting – so very tempting . . . and yet worth so little compared to what he was being offered.

He opened the soundproof vault with the cardkey he had taken from Wallace. The R6 was behind an inner door, each small lump of metal in its own jar. It was perfectly safe of course . . . still, there was no point in taking more chances than necessary. Da Silva opened his case. The upper section housed the sound suppressor. Beneath that, there was a soundproof compartment big enough to hold six of the jars. He held it open with one hand, while with the other he reached to open the inner door –

The alarms wailed out.

For one second, Da Silva considered risking it: taking the R6 and hoping that it would be safe for the few seconds it took him to transfer it to his case.

Stupid idea. He needed time and he needed silence.

He slammed the case shut, knowing that any minute now some fool of a security guard would be playing the hero. His feet made no sound as he darted towards the stacks of gold.

Voices echoed out round the warehouse. Two of them, coming closer. He saw them silhouetted against the light – saw them stop in front of the soundproof chamber.

Keep looking at it, he willed them. Keep worrying about your jobs. He slipped away, out of the vault, across the courtyard, over Wallace's prone body, through the gate and away.

He ran a little way, then forced himself to slow to a walk. His body sang with the adrenalin surging through it. This was it, this was living, this was the thing that sheepmen like Raymond Charlesworth could never understand.

It almost made his failure into a success: after all, now he had an excuse to make another, even more daring, attempt on the R6.

Ros nibbled on a corner of toast. Even after a good night's sleep, it was the most she could face.

Ed wandered in, fresh from an early morning run. 'How's the patient today?' he asked. He glanced at her plate. 'What, no bacon and eggs?'

The very thought made her stomach queasy. 'I may never look at another vegetable again,' she said. 'But I'll be all right with a few days rest.'

'Better plan on taking it some other time,' Beckett said from the doorway. He held up a fax. 'We've got another job.'

'Great,' Ros said. She sighed. Oh, well, she thought. At least it was a good excuse not to eat any more breakfast.

Beckett had had a bad feeling from the first moment he'd realised he wasn't to be briefed by anyone from Millennium Metals, but rather by an outsider – someone from the government.

The bad feeling had only got worse when she'd told him which department she was with and what her rank was. It roughly translated to 'government fixer, first class'. As he'd pointed out to Ros and Ed, just before they parted company – they were going to take a preliminary look at the security arrangements – he'd had trouble with that department when he was in the Hive; and the higher up its operatives got, the more arrogant they became.

Georgina Kent did nothing to make him change his mind. She was tall and severe-looking, with her hair pulled back into a chignon off her face and a cut-glass accent that suggested the very best education.

Beckett lounged back in his chair, determined to make the point that if they were to do the job, they couldn't and wouldn't be beholden to outside agencies.

'How much do you know about metal development, Beckett?' she asked.

'A little,' he answered, not bothering to tell her that he knew as much as he'd been able to learn from the in-car computer database on the way over.

Kent waved a gloved hand at what could be seen through the smoked glass of the office's interior window. 'This place operates under government licence to develop new metals and alloys for various applications –'

'I gathered as much,' Beckett said; his enquiries had indicated that it was one of the few such places whose basic research was not targeted primarily at military applications.

'Some very secret advances have been made here recently – advances which could have major implications for our economic future –'

'In particular?' Beckett asked, trying not to sound too interested. He'd gone to lengths to get free of the Hive; he wasn't keen to get tangled up in official machinations again.

'A new metal called R6. It will be an extremely efficient superconductor – my department has high hopes for it.' She paused. 'Unfortunately, it also has certain other properties.' Again, she paused, and this time it was obvious to Beckett that she was trying to decide how much to tell him. 'It's rather unstable . . .'

Translation, Beckett thought: this R6 had numerous possible uses, but at the moment it was nothing much more than an explosive. Kent's department wanted first dibs on it, and they didn't want the military or the intelligence services grabbing it.

No wonder they'd hired Gizmos rather than making the enquiry official.

Ed stared at the video monitor. The date on the tape said it showed the night before, about eleven pm. The screen showed a guard walking across the courtyard, doing his rounds. He stopped in front of the camera and gave a thumbs-up to his mates. They'd have been in this room – security control. Even now, security staff were manning the monitors while he and Ros worked at a desk in the corner.

That must have been at about the time of the break-in – yet the tapes didn't show it, or the explosion.

Any minute now, Ros would reverse the tape, as she had three times already. Ed didn't know how she had the patience.

Sure enough, her finger jabbed out and pressed the controls on the Gizmos video analyser she was playing the tape through. The tape went into fast rewind, to well past the shot of the guard. Stopped. Went forward again, this time in slow-mo.

'Someone's been playing home videos,' she said. A white band flickered across the screen. 'Look – an interruption to the signal.' She fast-forwarded again. 'Where's that shot of the guard?' She jogged the tape forward. The guard walked past the camera and did his thumbs-up. Ros hit freeze-frame. 'Here he is – fit and well.'

'And now he's unconscious in hospital,' Ed said. He sat down and rubbed his eyes, trying to think it through. 'Are you saying that's not Wallace?'

'Oh, that's Wallace all right,' Ros said. She enlarged the picture, then did it again and again, until the monitor was filled only with the image of a newspaper sticking out of his jacket pocket. 'But that's not yesterday's paper.'

'An old recording,' Ed said.

'Someone's interrupted the video feed from the security cameras and fed this to the recorder instead.' Ros clicked off the video recorder.

Ed ran his hand through his hair. 'That's a heck of a lot of trouble to go to not to steal anything.' And heaven only knew, he thought, there was enough worth stealing in the Millennium Metals vault. One bar of platinum would be worth thousands, at least. 'And then there's the other weird thing,' he added. 'The guards say they never heard the explosion.'

'Actually, there's a reason for that,' Beckett said. Ed turned round. He hadn't heard Beckett come in. The government contact, Georgina Kent, was standing next to him. She was a tall redhead in a severe suit and an even more severe hair-do. 'Something you should know about this R6,' Beckett finished.

'It makes people deaf?' Ed hazarded.

'Not exactly,' Beckett said. He looked expectantly at Kent.

'I've asked Mr Vermeer to explain – after all, he is their vice-president.' Kent said. 'If you'd like to step this way?'

She led them out of the security control centre and down to a small laboratory. As they walked, Ed considered asking her out to dinner. She was a bit old for him, but that wasn't too important. Then he remembered the imperious way she'd looked at them, and her voice, which was clearly used to giving orders and having them obeyed, and he decided he wouldn't stand a chance.

Come to think of it, he couldn't imagine the man who would.

Obediently, he filed into the laboratory behind the others. Mr Vermeer was waiting for them. He was a grey man in a grey suit, and he stared at them stonily as they sat down.

He nodded to a technician, who placed a glass tumbler in a transparent containment chamber on the far side of the room.

'Watch,' Vermeer said. He took out a small black box from which an aerial protruded, and pointed it at the tumbler. A high-pitched whine shrieked through the room. It was almost unbearable to start with – like a fingernail scraped down a never-ending blackboard – and it got louder and louder.

The tumbler exploded.

No one touched it, Ed thought. The chamber was empty. I know it was. He got up to have a closer look.

'Resonant frequency,' Ros said, as if that explained everything.

Ed chewed his lip. It was clear from the expression on Beckett's face that he either understood what Ros was talking about or – more like – he'd had a fuller explanation earlier on.

'Hang on a second,' he said. He hated these moments when he had to ask for explanations. 'I never did much physics at school – I was more into human biology.' He glanced at Kent. She stared back coolly. Scratch that, he thought.

'Ed,' Ros said, though whether she objected to him

eyeing up a client or admitting he didn't understand something in front of outsiders, he wasn't quite sure. 'At the correct frequency the glass absorbs so much energy that it explodes. Okay?'

Ed nodded, still not a hundred per cent sure.

'And the same thing happens with R6,' Beckett added.

Smartarse, Ed thought.

Vermeer graced Beckett with a smile. 'Something similar.'

'Only R6 is more volatile,' Kent added. She nodded, and another technician came forward – only this one was dressed from head to toe in Kevlar protective clothing, and was wearing heavy gauntlets and a full face mask. He – Ed presumed it was a he, though it was impossible to tell – was carrying a crucible in which there was a lump of silvery metal about as big as the first joint of Ed's thumb. He put it in the containment chamber and closed the door.

Vermeer did something to his device. 'Ready?' he asked.

Everyone nodded. He pointed the device at the nugget of metal. This time the shriek was even higher-pitched, though not as loud in volume.

The metal exploded like a thunderflash, in a ball of flame and smoke.

For a moment there was silence.

Ros broke it. She was clearly impressed. 'You can mould this stuff?' she asked.

Vermeer nodded. 'Oh yes – it's quite malleable, and stable with the one exception of the resonant frequency.'

'So you could make some innocent metal object from R6 – like a fountain pen – and send it to your least favourite national leader. Expose it to that resonant frequency and –'

'Bang!' Ed put in, picking up on her train of thought. 'Election time.'

'And no evidence of how it was done,' Beckett finished. That was typical of him, Ed thought – always looking for the devious angle, the problems others hadn't even anticipated, never mind prepared for.

'You can imagine how dangerous it could be if it fell into the wrong hands,' Kent said. 'You must ensure that doesn't happen.'

'We'll need full access to your existing security set-up,' Beckett said. 'Both here and at your research facility.'

Vermeer looked unhappy. Kent shot him a glance that said he *was* going to comply. His mouth tightened.

'We do have a very good security system here already,' he said.

Heard that one before, Ed thought. 'Wasn't up to much last night, was it?' he said.

Vermeer glared at him, then turned on his heel and left without speaking.

« Eight »

Ros mentally ticked off the list of modifications she wanted to make to the Millennium Metals security arrangements: motion-sensors, heat-sensors, the video cameras to be made tamper-proof . . .

Speaking of which, she wondered how Ed was getting on. She strolled over to where he was working on one of the perimeter cameras, at the top of a very tall ladder. Very tall, very wobbly.

He glanced down. 'Fancy changing places?' he called.

What she thought of that idea must have been written all over her face. 'I thought you liked heights?'

Ed shifted his weight as he tried to detach the video camera he was working on. The ladder moved under him. 'Tastes can change,' he said. 'Why do you want this, anyway?'

'I want to add a trick or two to the system,' she said.

Ed nodded, then gestured at the office block opposite. 'Ros – you see that place over there?' She looked where he was pointing – a large office block, all white walls and smoked glass windows, and separated from the rest of the industrial park by an expanse of water. 'You reckon their cameras might have picked something up last night?'

If they have cameras, she thought. 'I don't know,' she said. She pulled her binoculars out of her holdall. The ruby coating on the lenses glinted in the sunlight. She looked through them; almost instantly the autofocus mechanism brought the building opposite into sharp relief. There was at least one camera pointing in the general direction of Millennium Metals, but that might not be good enough.

'Might be our best shot,' Ed said.

'They're in the right place,' she added.

Ed leaned down and reached for the binoculars. She handed them to him. He looked through them. 'Very interesting,' he said.

'I'll tell Beckett to get over there,' Ros said.

'Uh, Ros? No need for that.' Ed handed back the binoculars. 'I can handle this one,' he finished.

Ros glanced at the other building. Even without the binoculars she could clearly see a pretty young woman going back inside the building, with a package she must have just taken from a motorbike courier.

Ros grinned wryly at Ed. I'm sure you won't have any problem there, she thought.

Ed gave the receptionist he'd seen through the binoculars his best smile. She was blonde and blue-eyed, and exquisitely pretty.

She listened attentively while he explained about the break-in.

She smiled. It was enough to stop the breath in Ed's throat, and for a moment he thought his luck was in, in more ways than one.

'No, I'm afraid it's impossible,' she said.

'If we could take a look at those tapes, it would be a major help to our investigation.' He was making eye

contact with her now. Just as well he'd come over –
Beckett would have tried to get heavy about national
security, and got absolutely nowhere.

What was needed was tact. Charm.

The receptionist's smile never wavered. 'It's company policy,' she said.

And persistence, Ed thought. He walked round the
desk to get closer to her. 'You could keep your eye on
me the whole time,' he said. He was close enough to
smell her perfume, now. He perched on the edge of her
desk. 'Personally.'

She stood up, still smiling. 'I'm sorry,' she said. 'The
head of security is very strict. When they change the
tapes, Mr Thomas insists they go straight in the safe.'

Of course, Ed thought, there was such a thing as
knowing when you were beaten. 'Very sensible,' he
said. She was probably a bottle blonde anyway. 'I
suppose they change the tapes frequently, do they?'

'Eight o'clock each night, on the dot,' she answered.
'Mr Thomas says our system is state-of-the-art.'

Yep, Ed thought as he left the building; but not the
state of Ros's art, that was for sure. His eye lit on the
company logo etched into the plate-glass door: Rimmington Refrigeration.

No wonder they employ ice maidens, he thought.

Da Silva leaned back in his chair – or, rather, Charlesworth's chair – with his feet on the desk and watched
Charlesworth pace up and down in front of him.
Doubtless the grey man thought he was a lion rest-
lessly pacing the confines of his cage; but to Da Silva
he looked like a mouse scurrying pointlessly to and
fro.

Charlesworth stopped. 'What do you mean, it wasn't
a failure?' he said. A fleck of spittle flew from his
mouth and was lost in the bright air. 'You didn't get

131

the R6 – in what sense is that not a failure?' He slammed his hand down on the desk.

Da Silva said lazily, 'In the sense that it's the perfect diversion.'

Charlesworth licked his lips. 'If you say so,' he said.

'Let me take care of – what shall I call it – matters arising out of last night. Then I'll get your R6. I promise.' He took his feet off the desk and leaned forward. 'You do trust me, don't you?'

'Well ... yes. Of course,' Charlesworth said, clearly flustered.

Then you're a fool, Da Silva thought.

Ed crossed the walkway leading across the water to Rimmington Refrigeration.

He found a shadow cast by the wall and waited there. A security guard came round the corner. I'm just out for a quiet stroll, Ed thought at him. That's all I'm doing, just waiting in this nice dark shadow as part of my evening constitutional.

The guard disappeared round the side of the building. As soon as he was out of sight, Ed vaulted over the railings, ignoring the awkward weight of the gear he was carrying across his shoulders.

He looked around. There was no one in sight.

State-of-the-art security, he thought. Yep. It was certainly in quite a state.

He checked his watch. The trouble with the tapes being changed at eight was that it didn't get dark till half past seven. Add in the need to avoid the security guard, and he was on a very tight schedule.

The sheer side of the Rimmington Refrigeration building stretched up in front of him. Ed pulled the climbing gear off his shoulders: a power grapnel and line, attached to a pair of climbing handles, then he hissed into his headset mike: 'I'm in position.'

'We're ready when you are, Ed,' Ros said. He could just imagine them, sitting in Beckett's nice warm car while he froze out here in the cold.

Still, there was nothing like an adrenalin rush to get the blood moving.

He put the climbing handles on the ground and aimed the grapnel at a protruding ledge near the top of the building. He stepped on the climbing handles to hold them down, then pressed the button on the canister. The grapnel shot upwards, with just a hiss from the gas cylinder to break the quiet of the night.

The line the grapnel trailed was almost invisible against the white building. Ed tugged on it. It seemed secure enough. He attached the canister holding the rest of the line to his safety belt, then pressed the wind button.

The line drew him smoothly upwards, reeling into the canister as he went. His feet kicked gently against the side of the building. The world fell away beneath him.

He came up next to the camera, and locked the line in place. All he had to do was attach the box of tricks Ros had given him to the side of the camera – she'd do the rest by remote.

'Quick as you can, Ed,' Ros said.

He got the device out of his jacket pocket.

'You've got ... sixteen minutes till they change the tapes,' Beckett said.

'All right, all right,' Ed said. 'You want to come up here and see if you could do it any quicker?'

That was mean, he thought, as he fumbled with the device, trying to get the side with the magnetic strips against the camera. He'd never seen Beckett look so green as when they'd been going up and down on top of the lift at the Hennessey-Brock skyscraper.

And, Ed thought, he had something solid under his feet then.

133

'How's it going, Ed?' Ros asked.

'No worries,' he said.

The device slipped out of his hand. It lodged against the camera bracket for a moment, then fell.

He caught it.

'Don't say a word – not a thing,' he said, then realised they wouldn't have known anything about it if he'd kept quiet. 'Everyone's a critic,' he muttered to himself as he finally managed to secure the box to the camera. 'Okay, Ros – I've attached it,' he said. 'Start recording now.'

He settled down to wait, enjoying the feeling of freedom that hanging in the air brought.

'Can we get it all down before they change tapes?' Beckett asked. His voice came over Ed's headset loud and clear, though he was obviously talking to Ros.

I certainly hope so after all this, Ed thought.

'I'm speed-recording at a ratio of a hundred to one,' Ros said. 'I need fourteen minutes and twenty-four seconds.'

Ed glanced at his watch. By his reckoning, she was going to lose the last half a minute or so – however long that was in real-time.

He stared at the lights shimmering on the water, and beyond that the city, its neon glow glittering in the darkness like diamonds on a jeweller's tray. Among them, he thought he could pick out the dark shape of the Hennessey-Brock tower, in the heart of the financial district. Three miles or so beyond that, lost in the myriad of lights, would be the Gizmos office. Poor old Beckett, he thought – it would be a shame to get such vertigo that you could never appreciate a sight like this.

But it did pall after a bit. Especially when he started getting cramps in his calf muscles.

'Wish I'd brought something to read,' he muttered.

'Quiet, Ed,' Beckett said. 'Company.'

Ed glanced down. A guard and his dog were walking along the side of the building. Taking their time about it, too.

Go chase a cat or something, dog, Ed thought. He flattened himself against the side of the building. Mustn't move, he thought. Not a muscle. Not an inch.

But he couldn't resist a quick glance down. The guard was standing directly beneath him, flashing his torch backwards and forwards and into the lobby of the building – everywhere but up. The dog cast around. It seemed to pick up a scent.

'I can almost hear your heart pounding, Ed,' Beckett said.

Thanks a bundle, Ed thought.

He risked another look. The dog was straining towards the gate.

'You daft ...' the security guard said. 'Come away, Radar ... come away now.' The dog hesitated, then stopped pulling at its leash. 'You daft bugger,' the guard said. 'You're supposed to find people breaking in, not going out.' He fondled the dog behind its ears. 'Time we were getting on.' He walked off.

Well good for you, Radar, Ed thought. He let himself relax a little.

After a while he said, 'Are you sure you're using the fast-forward?' He felt like he'd spent most of his life dangling against this building, with the possibility of a security guard and his far brighter dog finding him at any second.

'I'm going as fast as –' Ros said, and broke off. '– Oh no!'

'What's up?' Ed asked. Not more company, he thought. Knowing his luck, the next guard that came round the corner would have the wit to look up as well

135

as straight ahead. Or pay attention to his dog.

'They're changing the tape,' Ros said. 'Someone must have wanted to go home early.'

'Let's hope we've got enough,' Beckett cut in.

'Ed – you might as well come down,' Ros said. She didn't sound amused.

Ed detached the device – it was far easier to pull it off than it had been to put it on the camera in the first place – and released the lock on the power line.

He bounced his way down to the ground far faster than he'd gone up – it wasn't so different from ordinary abseiling. The instant his feet touched the ground he pulled the power line canister from his belt and attempted to retrieve the grapnel. In a way, this was the trickiest part of the whole operation.

It took him three goes to get the right flick of his wrist, and all the time he was watching, watching for the security guard. Or more to the point, his dog.

At last the grapnel unhooked itself from the ledge. It fell towards him. He stepped aside and caught it deftly, before it could land.

He sprinted towards the gate and vaulted over it.

Sounds behind him.

He dived to one side. The shadows engulfed him just as the security guard came back round the corner.

Absolutely nothing wrong with me being here, he thought. Nothing illegal in it at all. Nothing they can pin on me, anyway.

Again, the dog started to cast around in the direction of the gate. Again the security guard called it off. As they carried on with their round, Ed walked away.

Next time, listen to Radar, he thought.

After all, next time it might be a bad guy.

There was nothing quite so wonderful to Ros as a piece of technology that worked – unless it was a piece of technology that worked and solved a problem that had been bothering her.

She worked on the Rimmington Refrigeration tapes all night at Gizmos, and by the next morning she had a couple of things to show Ed and Beckett.

'Look at this,' she said, palming sleep out of her eyes. 'It's incredible.'

Ed leaned against the desk behind her. Beckett pulled up a chair. Ros played the tape. It was silent, of course, and in grainy black and white. A security guard patrolled the Rimmington Refrigeration building. He met with another man and stood talking by the wall that overlooked the water. Behind them, the Millennium Metals vault door blew up. Neither of them so much as looked round.

Ros looked expectantly at Beckett. He didn't say anything. She looked at Ed.

'So?' he said.

'Look at the foreground,' Ros said.

'A couple of security guys,' Ed said. His tone said he was unimpressed. Ros wasn't surprised, considering how easy he found it to run rings round them.

Ros rewound the tape. 'There's the explosion,' she said. 'You see the cloud of debris? But look at *them*.'

'No reaction at all,' Beckett said.

Ros grinned in triumph. 'Exactly,' she said, turning round in her chair to face them. 'The Millennium Metals guards were right – there was no sound. The explosion was silent.'

Ed frowned. 'Ros – how do you attach a silencer to a lump of MDX?'

'You don't,' she said. 'Not physically. But there's been a lot of work on sound-suppression recently –'

'Like Stross Cybertech is working on?' Ed asked. 'Wasn't that one of the things he mentioned in his message?'

'Good point,' Beckett said. 'But I thought that was just small-scale stuff – car phones, stereos –'

'If that was all there was to it, you can bet Charlie wouldn't be interested,' Ros said. 'The theory goes that every noise has its own frequency pattern, right?' Ed nodded uncertainly. It was obvious that Beckett was way ahead of him. 'Which means that if you can create the negative image of that sound and transmit it at the same time as the noise is created, then one cancels out the other.'

'Result: silence,' Beckett said. He looked at Ed. 'You want to see if you can get hold of Charlie?'

'Why?' Ed asked. 'We don't need to know any more theory, do we?'

'No,' Ros said, realising where Beckett was heading. 'But maybe someone's bought one of these things off Charlie recently – and if not, he's bound to know who else is working in the same field.'

Ed nodded. 'Right,' he said. He started to go.

'Hang on,' Ros said. 'There's one more thing I'd like you to see.' She fast-forwarded to the section she'd marked. It clearly showed the gate being opened to let in a swarthy-looking man dressed all in black. 'See?' she said. 'It was an inside job.'

Ed got up and peered at the screen. 'But that's the guard who ended up in hosptial.' He thought for a second. 'What's his name? Wallace.'

'Best cover,' Beckett said. 'Takes the pressure off him.' Ros raised her eyebrows at him. She didn't know much about what Beckett had got up to before they met. At times like this, she didn't want to. 'Right now he's our best lead – I'll pay him a visit.'

'And I'll contact Charlie Stross,' Ed said.

They both looked at her expectantly. 'And I'm going to get some sleep,' she said. 'I've been working on that tape all night.'

In the event, she didn't get much rest. She was napping in the back office when Ed woke her. She pushed herself into a sitting position.

He sat down on the arm of the sofa she was sleeping on and said, 'I just phoned the Sci-Tech hotel where that seminar's being held – and Charlie checked out early yesterday morning. The receptionist remembered he said he was ill.'

'Yes, people do tend to remember Charlie, don't they?' She felt distinctly fuzzy from being woken up. 'Anyway what's the problem?'

'I just phoned Stross Cybertech. He hasn't phoned in since the day before yesterday,' Ed said. Before Ros could interrupt, he went on: 'And his wife says he didn't come home – I only hope I haven't worried her too much.'

It took Ros a second to take it all in through the haze of sleep. 'Wait a minute,' she said. 'You're saying you think he's been what . . . kidnapped?'

'Maybe,' Ed said. 'Or worse. Or nothing at all, if we're lucky.'

Ros's brain finally snapped into gear. 'No,' she said. 'I have a bad feeling about this.' She stood up. 'Come on,' she said. 'We've got work to do – this just got personal.'

« Nine »

Millennium Metals had paid for Wallace to be treated in Ravenbrook Sanitorium.

Walking through its landscaped grounds, Beckett could almost forget he was less than a mile from the crowded, polluted city centre. Gravel scrunched under his feet as he walked through an avenue of elm trees. He came out and crested a small rise. The hospital lay spread out below him, a large building faced in white and pale blue tiles. It was shaped like a circular pagoda, with each of its storeys smaller than the one below it.

Wallace's bill must have cost Millennium Metals a bundle, Beckett mused as he approached the entrance. If what he suspected were true, they were going to regret their generosity.

He went inside. The reception area was spacious, and filled with flowers and plants and deep sofas in soft grey leather. He went over to the reception desk and found that Wallace was in room 504, on the top floor.

He took the lift up. He was the only person in it, so he took the opportunity to set his mini-recorder to voice-activation. The disk was good for several hours of recording time, and he wanted to be sure he got everything Wallace had to say – the man might only be able to say it once, or he might clam up. Beckett didn't want to have to fiddle with the recorder and lose his only chance.

The corridor the lift opened onto was totally different from the reception area: its bare walls and hard floors almost shouted efficiency, and the universal disinfectant smell of hospitals was pervasive.

There were a few nurses around, one or two patients, no one that looked like a visitor; but that was okay – the hospital had an open visiting policy. Still, best to be circumspect, he thought – you never knew who might be taking an interest in Wallace's visitors. Besides, he didn't want some nurse telling him not to upset her patient. He slipped straight past the nurse on the desk while she was writing something in a log book.

He entered Wallace's room without being challenged, and shut the door behind him. The man lay in bed with his eyes shut. A drip led from a saline bottle to his arm, and a monitor beeped at regular intervals.

Beckett went and pulled up one of Wallace's eyelids. The iris didn't respond to light, so he was well under.

That sent questioning him out the window, Beckett thought. Still, it wasn't all bad news. He rifled quickly through the bedside drawer, looking for anything that might reveal the identity of Wallace's mystery employer. Nothing. Nothing in his holdall either. Stands to reason, Beckett thought grumpily; he supposed someone would have had to bring things in for him.

That left one thing for him to do. He reached into his jacket pocket and pulled out a small anti-static bag containing two electronic bugs. He found Wallace's shirt in a cupboard, and fixed one of them under the collar.

Before he was done, there was a noise from outside the door. Beckett's head jerked round. The doorhandle turned.

'I'm just going to change Mr Wallace's drip,' said a female voice.

There's nothing wrong with me being here, Beckett thought, though habit and instinct made him look for a hiding place. He dropped the shirt, figuring out his story as he did so.

The handle moved back up. 'Mrs Jones, you must go back to bed,' said the nurse, as if she were talking to a child. Her footsteps clattered away down the hall.

Beckett didn't wait. He darted round to the other side of the bed and rummaged through Wallace's holdall again. It had a hard bottom. Beckett lifted it up and slid the bug under it, then put it back. He piled Wallace's things back into the bag – they'd been pretty disorganised, and he didn't think Wallace was in any position to know what had been where.

He stared at his handiwork for a moment. Good enough, he thought, and walked out of the room as if he had a perfect right to be there.

He went past a few patients and one or two doctors and nurses on his way back to the lifts. As he passed the desk, he saw one of the nurses staring at the retreating back of the doctor he had just passed. Oh come on, he thought – he's not that good-looking.

Then he heard her say to her colleague, 'I don't know how the hospital expects to get any continuity of care –'

'Not with all these different doctors they keep getting in,' her colleague agreed. 'Here today, gone tomorrow, some of them.'

Damn, Beckett thought. He turned and walked back

the way he'd just come until he was out of the line-of-sight of the desk. Then he ran.

He opened Wallace's door. Something was wrong, but he couldn't place it. Then he got it. The beep from the monitor had stopped.

He went across to the bed to have a better look. The canular had been pulled out of Wallace's arm, and the drip line was swinging –

Something hard whacked into his back. He slammed into the bed. A hand grabbed his hair and yanked him up. He got a glimpse of white sleeve before he was rammed against the wall. His head cracked against the plaster. He whirled round, trying for a straight-arm chop at his assailant. The man dodged back, then came in straight and low and planted his fist in Beckett's belly. Beckett grunted and doubled over. A hand slammed into the top of his face and he thumped back against the wall.

He couldn't breathe, couldn't move for pain, but he had to do something.

Again, the enemy hit him in the stomach. Again. The world blurred through the tears in Beckett's watering eyes.

His hands scrabbled for purchase against the wall. If he could get some leverage –

His exploring hand encountered the edge of something hard and boxy.

'You're going to have to do better than that, pal,' said the enemy.

Beckett looked up. Saw a swarthy Latinate face dominated by weird mirrored contact lenses. A fist came down at him. He managed to get one hand up, and with the other he hit the care-call button his fingers had just found.

An alarm whooped.

Beckett dodged just as the fist came down. The

Latino's hand slammed into the wall. He grunted, then turned and lunged for the door.

Beckett launched himself at the man's back. He grabbed his leather jacket, but the man shrugged him off and pelted down the hall towards a cross corridor.

Beckett raced after him. He crashed into a cleaning cart. Brooms and cloths went flying. He leapt over them and kept running.

'Get his drip,' he shouted at a startled-looking nurse. He turned and pointed.

He turned back. The enemy had disappeared.

He ran to the end of the corridor and glanced both ways. He was in luck. There was the enemy, silhouetted by light from the window at the end. He broke into a dead run, then launched himself at the man. They went barrelling into a trolley together.

'Better than this, huh, pal?' Beckett asked. He grabbed the man's arm and hauled him upright.

The man turned. 'This is outrageous,' he said.

Dark hair, pale skin. Nothing like Beckett's attacker. Beckett backed off.

Damn, he thought, and sprinted back the way he came, down the other leg of the T-junction to the lifts. There was no one in sight. He slammed his hand into the wall. A passing nurse raised her eyebrows at him and tutted in disapproval.

'Bad news,' he muttered.

He shoved open the door to the stairwell, but there was no one there. Pally was long gone.

Suddenly he realised how much he hurt. His shoulders felt like someone had cracked an iron bar across them, and his wrist throbbed.

As he made his way back to Wallace's room, he felt something in his pocket bumping against his hip. He shoved his hand in his pocket and found his mini-recorder. The green light was on, indicating that it was still recording. This might just be their first piece of luck. Beckett grinned but it quickly turned into a wince. He fingered his cheek gingerly. It felt like half a yard of skin had been taken off his face. It's just a scratch, he thought firmly.

The nurse was in Wallace's room, replacing his drip.

'Who was that man?' she asked.

'Uhh . . . friend of the family,' Beckett improvised. Not my best line, he thought as the nurse looked at him in confusion. 'They never did get on,' he added.

She smiled. 'We see a lot of that in here,' she said. She stopped what she was doing and peered at him. 'You're bleeding,' she said. 'Here – let me sort you out.'

Beckett sat on a chair and let her spray a dressing on. He wasn't in that much of a hurry, and she *was* pretty.

Besides, it would be something to tell Ed about.

« Ten »

Ros stared intently at the wave-form matrix displayed on her screen. Behind her, she could sense Beckett's presence. He was angry with himself for letting his attacker get away. It had been bad luck, nothing more, but Beckett demanded the same high standards from himself that he expected from others. Fortunately, he'd long since learned to save the recriminations for after a job was finished.

Not that she could blame Beckett for being angry – he'd taken quite a beating. The news that Charlie Stross might have fallen foul of the same man had added to his fury.

So now he leaned on her desk, glaring at the screen with all the intensity of a hunting falcon seeking its prey.

She clicked the 'play' button on the screen display.

'You're going to have to do better than that, pal,' said the man's voice through the speakers. The computer drew a graphic representation of the voice against its standard wave-form matrix. The voice played again. The computer refined its representation.

As the sequence repeated itself for the fifth or sixth

time, Ros saw Beckett's jaw clench. She supposed hearing that voice over and over again must be salting the wound. The failure would have hurt him as much as the beating, she knew. 'You sure you're all right, Beckett?' she asked.

'Yeah – I'm fine,' he said.

She let it drop, knowing she'd never get him to admit to needing a break. Before the voice could repeat again, she stopped it.

'That'll do,' she said. She fed the wave-table pattern into the scanning programme. 'The voiceprint will take a few seconds,' she said.

Meanwhile, she opened the C-ISDN modem link and selected a convoluted route through which to send her log-on request to the remote computer. Where she was going, she didn't want anyone following her home.

A couple of tense moments later, she'd hacked her way through the other computer's defences – log-in, user ID, password and all. 'Right,' she said, as the screen started to prompt her for information. 'Let's feed the voiceprint scan to their comparator program and see if they can find a match for it.' She fed the file she'd created a few moments earlier into the new system. 'Washington won't mind us using their files, will they?' she asked, all mock concern.

'Have you asked?' Beckett said.

'Don't usually,' she answered, and grinned. It was an old joke, almost a ritual they went through whenever they borrowed data from so-called secure systems around the globe.

There were footsteps behind her. She turned round. Ed walked in. 'Hey, Beckett,' he said. 'I hear you had him and lost him?' He slapped Beckett on the back. 'He did a good job on you –'

Beckett suppressed a wince. 'Yeah,' he said. 'But

you should see the other so-and-so.' He fingered the derma-patch on his cheek. 'And the nurse who fixed me up.' He grinned.

An alert box flashed on Ros's screen: 'Match found.'

'Guys?' she said. 'I've got something.' Instantly, Beckett and Ed were totally serious. 'Here we go,' Ros said.

A picture of a thin-faced, mousy man flashed up on the screen.

'Wait a minute,' Beckett said. 'That's not him.'

The caption read: 'Oliver Steinman; last known alias, Joseph Da Silva.' A brief biographical note said that he was a specialist in high-tech terrorism, and that his trademarks were electronics expertise and –

'Disguise,' said Ed. 'Known to use dermaplastic flesh-sculpting techniques . . .'

'That'll be our man, then,' Beckett said. Ros scrolled the screen. A list of names and places went by: North Vietnam (advisor to communist regime); Cambodia (CIA field officer); Chile (adviser to General Pinochet, special responsibility for elimination of rebel opposition); Israel (Six Day War – special adviser to General Dayan) . . . 'Looks like a freelance gun for hire.'

'Not fussy who he works for, is he?' Ros said as the screen continued to scroll. 'Argentina, Iran, Iraq, Nigeria . . . USA again, Russia . . .'

'I do like a well-travelled nutter,' Ed said.

Ros clicked to the next page of information. A screenful of thumbnail-sized pictures confronted her. Each showed a very different man. 'This explains a lot,' she said. 'Any of these look like him?'

Beckett nodded. 'That one,' he said, pointing to a picture of a swarthy, sallow-skinned man. Ros enlarged it, then sent it across to a graphics program running on one of the other Gizmos computers she was networked to. 'Is this more or less who we're looking for, then?'

she asked. 'Or do you want to change anything?'

Beckett studied the picture. 'Yeah,' he said. 'His features were kind of heavier ...' Ros made some changes. 'Better,' Beckett said. 'More on the eyebrows and ... that's it!' he exclaimed. 'He was wearing these mirrored contact lenses. You couldn't mistake them.'

Ros added them in. 'Take a good look, Ed,' she said. 'This is who we're after.'

'How do we find him?' Ed asked.

Beckett held out the headscanner. 'Wallace,' he said. 'There are two bugs on him, when he leaves hospital.' He handed the device to Ed.

'And in the meantime?' Ros asked.

'I'm going to see Kent at the research centre.' He started to go, but turned back before he got to the door. 'You go and see Vermeer – find out who else knows about R6.'

Someone had to, for sure. The real question is, Ros thought, have they hired Da Silva – or is he using them?

Ros and Ed followed Vermeer up the mirror-finished spiral staircase that led to his private office. Below them, Millennium Metals' front lobby was an acre of white marble trimmed in chrome and pale blue frosted glass. An ice-palace, Ros thought – that was what it reminded her of.

Come to think of it, the reception Vermeer had given them had been nothing short of frosty.

The stairs let out directly into his office. He walked straight over to his desk, but Ros paused for a moment, her breath quite stolen by what she saw.

The office was circular. It had no walls, only six arched windows that rose up and curved over to form a domed ceiling. A light source had been concealed behind the space where they met, and from this was suspended a slowly revolving pendant made of thousands of tiny slivers of crystal and glass. As they moved, they sent shadows and flashes of light darting across the white stone floor.

Totally impractical, she told herself as she followed Vermeer. Completely un-ergonomic: if it didn't give you migraine it would simply distract you, and if you forced yourself to concentrate you'd spend all day fielding questions about it from everyone.

She sat down next to Ed in front of Vermeer's desk. It was a sinuous curve of black marble. He stared at them expectantly, but didn't speak.

I could get to dislike that man very much, Ros thought. She wondered how long he'd let the silence continue.

In the end it was Ed who spoke first. 'Mr Vermeer, this was an inside job for sure.'

Vermeer steepled his fingers in front of him. 'What are you saying?'

'One of the security guards – Wallace – let the man in,' Ros said.

'I see.' Vermeer stared at them as if he thought they'd personally vetted the man and chosen someone unreliable. Ros felt like telling him that if they had carried out security checks on Millennium Metals' staff, the whole problem would never have arisen.

'We think there must have been another leak,' Ed said.

Vermeer just stared at him.

No wonder he likes all this stone, Ros thought. He behaves like his face is made of the stuff. 'The raiders knew what they were after – that's why they silenced their explosion,' she explained.

'Kent tells us R6 is highly secret,' Ed put in. 'Who else knows it exists?'

'Only a few of my most trusted employees,' Vermeer said. He unsteepled his hands and picked up his pen, as if to signal the end of the conversation. 'Oh!' he said, tapping the end of the pen on the desk, as if to punctuate a sudden thought. 'And Charlesworth, of course. I'd forgotten him.'

'Charlesworth?' Ed asked.

Vermeer scowled. It was the most emotion Ros had seen him display. 'He led the research team that discovered R6 by accident.'

Ros glanced back at Ed. His expression showed that he'd had the same thought she had. 'Can we speak to him?' she asked Vermeer.

'No,' he answered. 'He left our employ some time ago – we fell out over R6.' He opened a pewter-bound journal and wrote something down. After a second he looked up again, evidently having realised Ros and Ed hadn't left. 'We're trying to stabilise it so it can be used for what it was intended,' he said. 'But Charlesworth wanted to exploit its explosive nature as a weapon.'

Ros stood up. 'Thank you, Mr Vermeer,' she said. 'This has been most helpful.' She thought for a second. If Charlesworth really was behind the raids ... 'I don't suppose you'd have a picture of this Mr Charlesworth?'

'I'll tell Personnel to fax you a photo,' he said. 'Good day.'

As they left, Ed said, 'Would have been even more helpful if we'd known that to start with.'

'Yeah,' Ros agreed. She turned at the top of the stairs to take one last look at the office. 'There's just one more thing,' she said quietly.

'Uh huh?' Ed answered.

'This office – I want one just like it.'

Vermeer lay back on the couch in his office. It was his

regular therapy session, and his staff knew not to distract him.

'Relax,' said the therapist's gentle voice. 'Close your eyes if you want.' Vermeer did so. 'Last time,' the therapist said, 'we talked about your anger. What are you angry about this time?'

'Someone's stolen something valuable from me,' Vermeer said.

'Who do you think might have stolen something valuable from you,' asked the therapist.

'Charlesworth,' Vermeer said. 'It has to be him. The man has the morals of a weasel.'

There was a pause. Vermeer allowed himself the luxury of enjoying the sensation of thinking of nothing at all, of letting his muscles go limp and sinking into the couch.

'Why do you think Charlesworth has the morals of a weasel?' asked the therapist.

'He's just out for money. He doesn't care about anything else,' Vermeer said. 'I find that reprehensible – I pride myself on my integrity.'

'Why do you pride yourself on your integrity, Mr Vermeer?'

'Without it . . . without it we would have no society, no civilisation.'

'How do you know that without it we would have no society and no civilisation?' The therapist's voice was calm, rational.

'Because I had a proper upbringing,' Vermeer said. 'My father taught me that from an early age.'

'How did he teach you that from an early age?' the therapist asked.

'By making sure I never had anything I wanted, unless I was good,' Vermeer snapped. He remembered that so well – the lonely nights locked in his room, the Saturdays spent writing out chunks of Gibbon's

153

'Decline and Fall' instead of playing football or going to the cinema with his friends. Other punishments he wasn't – really wasn't – going to think about. 'Is it really any wonder that I'm angry?'

'Why are you angry, Mr Vermeer?' asked the therapist.

'Because I never have any fun, dammit,' Vermeer roared. 'Because now Charlesworth's going to get the money and I want it –'

'Why do you want it, Mr Vermeer?'

Vermeer's eyes snapped open. He stood up and strode over to the computer.

'Why do you want it, Mr Vermeer?' the therapist repeated in the same patient tone.

'Because I do, dammit. I just do – I want all the money, all for me.' He grabbed the mouse and clicked on 'Exit program'.

'This will end your therapy session,' said the therapist.

'Good,' Vermeer said.

He felt better than he had in years.

Moonlight mingled with the actinic glare from the security lights of the Millennium Metals Research Annexe. Most of the staff had gone home, and all was quiet.

A soft click sounded in the silence. The light glinted on the smooth metal of a service access cover set into the tarmac. Slowly it lifted up, then thudded back against the ground.

Joseph Da Silva hauled himself out of the service conduit. He reached back inside and pulled out a case. Like his clothes, it was matt black.

He looked around, orientating himself and relating what he could see to his map. Around him was a maze of low-built buildings, each plasticreted frontage almost identical to the one next to it. Only the colours differed, each one a code for a particular kind of research.

Yellow Block was to his right. According to his sources, that housed the division researching heat-resistant alloys for use in the space programme. To his left, Red Block: development of low-weight impact-resistant metals for military applications. At any other time, he might have been tempted ... but he needed Green Block, where work into the stabilisation of R6 was being carried out.

He sprinted down an alley between the two nearest buildings. Turned. Ran straight ahead. Green Block – two small buildings offset from the main research facility – appeared ahead of him.

The soundproof vault was the one to the left. Even if he hadn't known, the seals on the door would have told him.

He hid in the shadow of one of the red buildings opposite it and opened his case. He took out a MDX bomb and darted across to the soundproof vault with it. It was the work of a moment to attach it to the door.

He retreated to the shadows and set up the sound suppressor, then triggered the bomb. The door exploded silently.

Da Silva watched the rapidly dispersing cloud of smoke as he picked up the sound suppressor. He hurried into the soundproof vault. Inside, mounted on what Da Silva first took to be shock-absorbers but then realised were to isolate it from conducted sound, was a plain steel cube. Only a slight indent in its front panel indicated that it was, in fact, a safe.

He looked at it with contempt. If one door hadn't kept him out, did they really think two would?

Beckett watched the scientists at play. He couldn't help

thinking of it like that, though he knew they were deadly serious.

He was sitting in an observation room above one of the laboratories at the Millennium Metals Research Annexe. Below him, lit by flat, shadowless lighting, a woman in a white coat made minute adjustments to a series of devices attached to a bell-jar.

Any minute now, she was going to trigger the sound-emitting device that would explode the R6 in the bell-jar. He wished she wouldn't – his ears were still ringing from her last test.

He decided it was time to wind things up. He looked at his notebook. 'So,' he said, 'I've now seen all your precautions?'

There weren't very many of them. Perhaps his concern showed in his voice.

'There's really nothing to worry about,' Kent said. 'Our security here is really very good.'

'That's what Vermeer thought,' Beckett said. He really was finding it difficult to be patient with her. She'd never have employed amateur scientists, but she thought any amateur could take care of security. And when it all went wrong, she was sure to blame Gizmos, instead of her own lack of co-operation. He twisted round in his seat to confront her. 'You should have told me you had R6 here before.'

He stood up to go. There was really very little more to say.

'I didn't think it was relevant,' Kent said. She, too, got up.

'Of course it's relevant!' Beckett realised he was shouting and forced himself to lower his voice. 'If Da Silva wants it this badly, he'll go anywhere to get it.'

'Well he won't get it from here,' Kent insisted.

Beckett turned and walked away without saying

156

another word. There really wasn't any point.

Da Silva lifted the first of the jars of R6 out of its niche in the safe. Samples! That's all these were – barely enough R6 for a single small bomb in each jar, one that could kill just one person. Still, it was better than nothing. He placed it in his case, then took the others.

As he was putting the last one away, he heard a sound from outside. There was the distinct click of an opening door.

He'd had to leave empty-handed before. He wasn't going to let that happen again. He pulled his pistol out of his shoulder holster and hurried to the hole that was all that remained of the door. He slipped outside, and into the shadows between the two green buildings.

Beckett was having a hard time keeping his temper. Kent was still insisting the existing security precautions were adequate.

'Let me be the judge of that,' he said, as he followed her out through the door into the chill night air.

She headed towards the high-security vault in the next building. 'You'll see, Beckett,' she said. 'And anyway, I hired you to protect the R6 at the main installation, not interfere here –' Her head jerked round. She peered down the alley between the two buildings. 'Hey, you!' she shouted.

Beckett looked in the same direction. He had time to glimpse a swarthy face in the darkness. Light glinted on metal.

Then there was a quiet *whuff*. Kent yelped and staggered backwards, holding her chest. She toppled slowly. Beckett darted forward and caught her just before she hit the ground.

He heard a shoe scuff on the ground.

A dark figure ran past him, but all he could do was stare. He didn't dare leave Kent.

The figure paused for a moment. 'I said, do better than that, pal!' shouted a familiar voice.

Then the figure vanished into the darkness. Beckett looked down at Kent. Her face was deathly white, and blood was oozing between her fingers.

« Eleven »

Ros paced up and down the length of the Gizmos back office. Morning light slanted through the venetian blinds and striped the floor, so as she walked she went from light to dark to light again.

Beckett was standing near Kent, over on the other side of the room. They had turned up earlier that morning, having been at the local hospital all night.

Ros headed over in their direction, jiggling her earpiece to try and hear better as she walked. She was listening to Wallace via the bug that Beckett had placed on him. It was difficult to be sure, but it sounded as if he was walking down a corridor.

She raised her eyebrows at Kent. Clients being bumped off – even nearly bumped off – was bad for business.

'It's not nearly as bad as it looks,' Kent said. 'The doctor said if it had been a bullet it would have been a different story. As it is, it broke a rib and ruptured some skin and blood-vessels just under the surface.'

'So what was it?' Ros asked. She'd only had time to get the bare essentials of the story from Beckett before the bug monitor had beeped to let her know it was picking up activity.

'Puzzled me at first,' Beckett admitted. 'Then I remembered a conversation I had with Charlie when he first asked us to field-test the sound-suppressor –'

Ros nodded thoughtfully. 'I remember – something about non-lethal weaponry?'

'Yeah,' Beckett said. 'I reckon this wound was made by the shaped-sonic-charge pistol he told us about –'

'Could be,' Ros said. 'If so, then Charlie's either dead or in danger –'

'It seems this Da Silva is even more of a threat than we thought at first,' Kent said. She looked up at Beckett. 'And I owe you an apology – the Research Annexe was a target.'

Beckett started to say something, but just then a tinny voice in Ros's earpiece said, 'I'm sorry Mr Wallace – I've no instructions from the doctor about you leaving today.'

Ros made a shushing motion with her hand. 'Wallace is just getting himself discharged,' she said. She grabbed her coat.

'Right,' said Beckett. 'Let's go.'

They took Ros's car, and picked up Wallace's tail outside the hospital. He was in a taxi – a bright yellow one, which at least made it easy to follow.

While Ros drove, Beckett contacted Ed, who was doing some security modifications at Millennium Metals.

'Ed, Wallace is on the move. We're tailing him,' he said.

'Right,' Ed answered. 'I've almost finished here, and let me tell you, if Da Silva tries to get into Millennium Metals again, he's in for a big shock.'

'Good,' Beckett said. 'Hurry up and get mobile, though – we may need you out here.'

'Will do,' Ed said.

Beckett broke the connection and concentrated on spotting for Ros.

They drove north through increasingly leafy suburbs, and soon arrived at their destination.

'Very nice,' Ros said. 'The Riverbridge Hotel. I'll say this for Da Silva – if this is where he's staying, at least he's got a bit of class.'

'And someone else's money, I shouldn't wonder,' Beckett said. They waited in the car while Wallace got out of his taxi.

As its name implied, the hotel was built into a bridge across the river. It was made of smoked glass, and designed round three vast arches. A road ran straight over the top of the hotel, which was entered by way of lifts from the top and corridors that let out onto the embankment at either side.

'Okay,' Beckett said. He got out of the car and headed for the lifts.

Ros wasn't following him. He turned back. She was arguing with a man in hotel livery. He had his hand out. Tip? Beckett wondered. But Ros was free with money . . . then he realised what it was.

He went back. 'Give him the key,' he said. Ros looked outraged. She treated that car the way some people treated their pet poodles. The thought of handing it over to a complete stranger was obviously too much for her. 'Valet parking,' he said as he took the keys from Ros and handed them to the attendant. She looked positively betrayed. 'He won't hurt it,' he said.

He turned and walked to the lifts as fast as he dared without attracting attention.

'But where's he going to put it?' Ros demanded.

'Car park's between the roof-street and the hotel,' he said. The lift arrived and they got in, only to find themselves infinitely repeated in its mirrored walls.

'Isn't it noisy?' Ros asked. She pulled the tracker out of her pocket.

'Not so you'd notice,' Beckett said. 'They obviously had a line on sound-proofing long before Charlie invented his suppressor.'

Ros nodded. 'How come you know so much about the place anyway – you aren't going to tell me you could afford it on the salary the Hive was paying you?'

Beckett smiled, but didn't answer. He knew how much Ros hated a mystery. 'We still all right?' he asked, indicating the tracker.

'Two more floors down, I think,' Ros said. After a moment she stopped the lift. They got out. She glanced at the tracker. 'That way,' she said, pointing ahead and to her right.

They set off down the corridor, their feet making no sound on the deep pile carpet. Outside, the sky was a rich blue, its colour deepened by the polarising glass of the hotel's walls.

'Here, I think,' Ros whispered. She pointed at one of the blondewood doors. Beckett nodded.

Ros padded forward and took a listening device from her pocket. She nodded after a moment, and went back to Beckett.

'Them?' he asked.

'Yeah,' she said. She went to the next door and listened at it. 'No good,' she said when she came back. 'Maid service is in there.'

'One above, then,' Beckett said. 'If I remember right . . .' He looked round till he found the door he wanted. 'Here we go,' he said. He opened the door. It led into the stairwell.

'What were you doing sneaking around the back stairs in a place like this?' Ros asked.

'Visiting a friend,' Beckett said, and suppressed a

grin as she got in a mess trying not to look curious and shocked at the same time.

They came out onto the next floor and located the room above the one Wallace was in. Luckily this time it was empty.

Beckett looked round quickly: luxury furniture, widescreen TV, fresh flowers on the sidetables, full-length windows with the drapes pulled back and a balcony beyond, doors leading to the other rooms of the suite. Rugs on the polished wood floor.

Beckett rolled one back while Ros fiddled with her listening device. She held her headphones off her ears so Beckett could hear too.

'Like I said, I want more money,' said Wallace's voice. 'You never said you were going to hurt me . . .'

'I'm sorry about this, Mr Charlesworth,' came Da Silva's thickly accented voice.

This time you're mine, pal, Beckett thought.

'Mr Charlesworth!' Wallace sounded genuinely startled. Beckett filed that piece of information in case it might come in useful. For one thing, it meant that Da Silva was working pretty much on his own initiative – but did that mean he considered himself Charlesworth's partner, with an equal right to make decisions? Or was this just a contract for him, one he would complete any way he could? The answers might make all the difference to what he would do and how he should be handled.

'I told you no one must –' Charlesworth said. He paused, then said, 'Deal with this, and meet me later.'

'You don't want to trust this one, Mr Charlesworth – he'll only try and cheat you,' Wallace said.

'This won't take long,' Da Silva said.

It was clear to Beckett what he meant. He wondered if Wallace realised.

'No more foul-ups,' Charlesworth said. There was

the double click of a door opening and closing.

'I'll get Ed to check him out,' Beckett said. He sprinted through the door, along the corridor and down the stairs. He opened the door at the bottom a crack, convinced he was too late. Luck was with him – perhaps the conversation had continued for a moment. A man – presumably Charlesworth – was just coming out of Da Silva's room. He headed for the lifts.

Beckett closed the door and radioed Ed. 'Where are you?' he asked, as he walked back upstairs.

'The hotel lobby,' Ed said. 'I've just arrived.'

'Well, don't get too comfortable – I've got a job for you. Charlesworth should be heading for his car – stick with him.'

'Will do,' Ed said.

Beckett broke the connection just as he went back into the room where Ros was. 'Ed's seeing to him,' he said.

'Shh!' she said. 'I'm trying to listen.' There was a muffled bang. Ros winced and tore her headphones off. 'Gunshot!' she said.

She leapt up and grabbed her holdall.

Beckett stared at the window. He hesitated for half a heartbeat. 'I'll take the window,' he said.

Demons were to be conquered.

'I'll take the stairs,' Ros said.

The windows slid aside at Beckett's touch. He went out onto the balcony. Like the rest of the hotel's structure, it was made from solid smoked glass, but unlike the rest it was intricately carved.

He looked over the edge. A hundred feet below, the river ran by; its surface was ruffled by the wind and silvered by the failing, westerly sun, and revealed nothing of its depths.

Fall into that and they'd never find you. Not alive, anyway.

He took a deep breath. Another. Then he hoisted himself up on the edge of the balcony, turned round and – before he had time to change his mind – lowered himself over the edge.

His heart was pounding. His feet kicked against the outside of the balcony. He lowered himself further. To think Ed did this for fun . . .

His feet kicked again, and again, and then met only air.

Against his best intentions, he felt himself start to panic. His hands were sweating. Slippery. What would Ed say about this? Hang on to anything you can. Don't look down. Keep three points of contact at all times.

Well, he'd already screwed up the last one, and he wasn't doing too well on the first . . .

His fingers closed over a bit of carving. He grabbed on to it. Lowered himself a little further. Felt the top of the lower balcony's rail beneath his feet.

One chance, he thought. He swung in. Got his feet inside the lower balcony and let himself drop.

For one vertiginous moment he felt himself topple backwards. Then he managed to grab the balcony and he was down.

He wanted, very much, to go somewhere quiet and throw up. Instead, he slid open the balcony door and went inside. Wallace's body was sprawled just inside the door. There was a sound outside. Ros. He stepped across Wallace and let her in.

'Over here,' he said, and turned to show her. She followed him. He put his hand to the pulse point on Wallace's neck, though the spreading blotch of blood at his temple told its own story. 'He's dead,' he said.

One of the internal doors crashed open. Da Silva raced out, grabbed Wallace's holdall and sprinted for the door. Ros launched herself at him. He flailed at her and caught her across the side of the head. She slammed back into the sofa, and he dived out of the door.

It banged shut behind him.

'Not again,' Beckett snarled. He slammed his hand into the wall. He looked at Ros. 'You okay?'

'My turn to say I'm fine,' she said. 'Come on.'

They ran outside. The stairwell door was standing open. It hadn't been before. Beckett went through it cautiously. If he hadn't been convinced that Da Silva was a stone-cold killer, he was now.

But he was nowhere in sight. Beckett looked up – he had to be heading for the car-park.

'Down!' Ros said. She clattered down the stairs ahead of Beckett. Suddenly she pulled the tracker out of her holdall. It was bleeping rapidly. 'It's okay,' she said. 'The bug's still in Wallace's bag – we've got him.'

Beckett said, 'I'm not letting him get away again. Not this time.' He saw a flash of black leather jacket. 'That way,' he said, heading for the door back into the corridor.

As they entered it, Da Silva disappeared round a corner at the end. Beckett broke into a dead run, pushing aside a maid with a laundry cart. He turned the corner and came out into the lift area. Da Silva was nowhere in sight.

'Up,' Ros said.

Beckett slammed his hand against the call button. He'd have used the stairs, but there was no way they'd make it up thirteen flights before Da Silva.

The lift arrived mercifully quickly.

'Lobby or car-park?' he asked Ros, once they were inside.

'Car-park,' she said. 'But get ready to stop the lift if this thing says to.' She hefted the tracker.

While they were going up, Ed radioed in. 'I'm

following Charlesworth,' he said. 'I managed to get a bug on his car.'

'How'd you manage that, then?' Beckett asked.

'Impersonated a car jockey,' Ed answered. 'It's probably illegal but –'

'I wouldn't sweat it,' Beckett said. 'Da Silva's just murdered Wallace.'

'Great,' Ed said. 'I'll talk to you later.' He broke the connection.

'Looks like my hunch was right,' Ros said. 'We've just passed the lobby level and the tracer wants us to keep going.'

Beckett nodded. 'Better turn the audio off,' he said. 'No point warning him we're coming.'

Ros flicked a switch and the bleeping stopped.

The lift doors opened a moment later, and they went out.

The car-park stretched out around them, rank upon rank of vehicles receding into the distance.

'Over there,' Ros said, showing Beckett the direction-finder on the tracker. 'He's not moving . . . could be a trap.'

They went forward cautiously.

Too much cover, Beckett thought. Too many cars, too much shadow, not enough light.

He heard a sound behind him.

Whirled, ready to throw himself and Ros to the ground.

Nothing.

His throat was dry. There was a cold knot in his belly. How many times had he done this kind of thing? It didn't matter. It never got any easier.

A faint hum started up behind them. He turned. So did Ros. In the distance, the doors of the car-park lift slid slowly open. An engine started up. Then he spotted the car. He started to run towards it, but it was useless.

It entered the lift, and the doors closed behind it.

'That's that, then,' he said. He was completely unable to keep the disgust out of his voice.

Ros laid her hand on his arm. 'Beckett,' she hissed. 'He's still here.' She pointed with the tracer. 'That way,' she said.

If they'd been cautious before, now they were cat-like. A bright flash of yellow stood out from the massed ranks of cars.

Ros's car? Beckett thought wonderingly. Maybe Da Silva had more resources than they had thought. He indicated for her to go one way, while he went the other. He dropped to a crouch and scuttled forward, hiding behind the car next to Ros's. Ros did the same on the other side.

He peered under the car. Nothing. He stood up, feeling slightly foolish. Oh well, he thought. Better red than dead.

He went round to the back of the car and met Ros. Wallace's bag was sitting on the bonnet. There was a note pinned to it.

Beckett picked it up and read it out: ' "I said you'll have to do better than that, Pal".' He slammed it back onto the holdall. 'That bas –'

'Don't you think you're making this too personal?' Ros asked.

Beckett stared at her for a long moment, then looked away. 'I suppose so,' he said.

'Let's get back to Millennium Metals and see what we can do there,' Ros said. She started to open the car door.

Ros's car, Beckett thought. *Ros's* car. 'Don't!' he said, as it all fell into place. 'Just back off slowly,' he said.

They'd been through too much together for her not to do it. She took her hand off the door and moved away. 'What is it?' she said.

'Why your car? Why not just dump the bag?' Beckett asked.

Ros frowned. 'Rub your nose in it?'

'He's an explosives expert, remember?'

'You mean you think he's planted a bomb in *my car*?' Ros demanded hotly. 'You're right, Beckett – this *is* personal.'

Together they started a visual inspection of the car. Nothing obvious underneath. Nothing under the fenders or the wheel arches. Nothing inside.

'Only one place left,' Ros said. 'The doors haven't been gimmicked so –'

'Under the bonnet,' Beckett said. 'Get back.'

'This is my fight too, Beckett,' Ros said.

She got between him and the car, so all he could do was leave her to it. She flipped up the bonnet. There, nestled to the starter motor, was a flat little pack that Beckett recognised as a DBX bomb.

'All right,' he said. 'I'll deal with it – you get as far away as you can.'

Ros shook her head. 'I'm better at this, and I'm defter,' she said. 'You warn them.'

Beckett took a deep breath. She was right, and he knew it. Besides, it was her car. 'All right,' he said. 'But I won't leave you – just in case you need me.'

He went and stood by a pillar several rows of cars away. Ros was a small, rather lonely figure, her white coat stark against the darkness as she bent over the car.

His radio crackled into life. 'Okay, Beckett,' she said. 'I've figured it out – I was scared it might be radio-controlled or on a timer, but it's wired into the starter motor instead.'

Silence. And nothing Beckett could do about it.

He wanted to hit something. Most especially, he wanted to hit Da Silva.

'Right,' Ros said. 'We're in with a chance – he didn't have a chance to do anything fancy in the way of booby-traps. All I have to do is make it think there's no break in the circuit and I should be able to disarm it.'

'Anything I can do?' Beckett asked.

'Yes,' she said. 'Shut up and let me concentrate.'

Time passed. Beckett couldn't have said how long. It felt like hours. It must have been minutes.

'Okay,' she said. 'I've got it – it's now attached to a permanently open switch that it thinks might deliver a current any moment, so it's a happy little bomb.'

'Not as happy as I am,' Beckett said. He broke the connection and went over to her.

She was leaning against the car, holding the bomb in one hand. 'There you go,' she said. 'Perfectly safe to be transported.' Her voice was trembling. So were her hands. Beckett smiled at her. He wanted to say something comforting, but it wasn't his way. Instead, he opened the car door. 'Your carriage awaits,' he said.

'Beckett?' Ros asked. 'You don't feel like driving, do you?'

« Twelve »

Ed tooled down the road behind Charlesworth's car. The traffic was thinning out and it was getting harder to stay inconspicuous. Ed dropped right back and relied on the bug. No reason to think it wouldn't work ...

He was glad he'd taken some precautions, as Charlesworth hung a sudden left and headed towards an abandoned industrial park towards the edge of the city.

Ed pulled over to the side of the road and got his binoculars out of his bike pannier. Sure enough, Charlesworth was entering the industrial park.

Ed set off again. This time he piled on a bit of speed. The anodised mesh of the park gates loomed ahead of him. Beyond them was a maze of factories, laboratories and office buildings.

Good enough, Ed thought. He'd had no intention of making a direct approach, and this just made things easier. He glanced at his tracker: Charlesworth was heading north by north-west.

Scratch that. He'd stopped about half a mile away. Ed swung the bike round to the left and threaded his way between two low-built buildings faced with blood-red tiles. Crossed an expanse of car-park, its security monitors long since smashed. Drove down a covered walkway between the two halves of a glass-fronted factory.

Ed pulled up just before the end of the walkway, where the bike wouldn't be easily seen. He swapped his helmet for his Gizmos headset, then set off for a quick recce of the area.

Ahead of him lay a white building, its boxy silhouette broken by several towers and domes. According to the tracker, Charlesworth – or rather his car – had to be nearby.

A lab of some kind, Ed decided. It was flanked on either side by other buildings. He skirted round it, using them for cover.

Charlesworth's car was parked outside.

'Beckett?' Ed whispered. 'You there?'

'Yeah,' Beckett answered, his voice made tinny by the radio.

'I've found out where Charlesworth was headed –'

'Good,' Beckett said. 'We lost Da Silva – he dumped the bag I bugged.' He paused. 'Now listen, Ed – I want you to check the place out, but no heroics –' He sounded tense. 'We've already had one nasty surprise from him today –'

'Oh yeah?' Ed said. He walked cautiously towards the building. Its windows winked blindly in the sun. He couldn't see anyone inside, but that didn't mean they couldn't see him.

'Just a little bomb scare,' Beckett said.

'What?'

'It's okay – we're both all right and no one was hurt. But don't take any chances, okay?'

'All right, Beckett,' Ed said. He continued his recce of the building. As far as he could see, there was just the one entrance. He looked up the wall: it was a total blank for the first fifty feet. If it came to a climb, he'd have to use crampons. He flicked his fingernail against it. It pinged.

Metal? he thought. Very interesting.

A car engine purred faintly in the distance. Ed dodged back into the cover of the next building. The sound grew louder. A car drew up.

The door opened and Da Silva got out. He walked straight into the front entrance.

Blast, Ed thought. Locating him in that place was going to take forever. He jogged back to the bike to get his gear, and activate his headset.

'Beckett?' Ed said. 'Guess who just turned up?'

'Da Silva?'

'Yep,' Ed said. The light glinting off the windows of the lab gave him an idea or two. He pulled out his binoculars and a piece of equipment that looked like a shoulder-mounted rifle with a small box on top; it had a pair of tiny earphones attached to it.

'Try and get a bug on them,' Beckett said. 'We need to know what they're planning. But don't do anything too impulsive – Da Silva's got the conscience of a piranha.'

'With any luck I won't be going anywhere near them,' Ed said. 'I'm going to try that laser-resonance bug. Talk to you later.'

He looked at the lab through his binoculars. The glare off the windows made it impossible to see any-thing. He flicked in the lens's polarising filters, then rotated them until the glare vanished and he was able to see inside.

Even so, it took him a few moments to locate Charlesworth and Da Silva. They were in one of the smaller domes. It was completely transparent, giving them almost 360 degrees of vision.

Ed grinned. They might be good, but he was better. He pulled his headset down round his neck and put the earpieces from the rifle on instead.

Then he raised the rifle to his shoulder, took careful aim and fired at the dome.

Nothing happened.

Nothing he could see, but he knew that a small spot of ruby light had appeared on the glass of the dome where his quarry was. Ros had explained it to him once – something about sound vibrations in the glass being transformed to electromagnetic radiation and transmitted back via the laser beam. Or something. Ed was more interested in the effect.

Which was that he could now hear every word Charlesworth and Da Silva said.

'Wallace?' Charlesworth asked.

'Dealt with.'

Ed could imagine how, though Beckett hadn't told him.

'Good,' Charlesworth said. 'We must get some of the R6 tonight – some of the sample from the research centre had first-level stabilisation. If the technique is perfected, the R6 will be useless to me.'

'I told you. You can trust –'

The voice suddenly stopped, to be replaced by a high-pitched squeal. Ed tore the earpieces out, wincing in agony.

He pulled his headset back on. 'Listen, there's something wrong with this laser bug – it died as soon as I activated it.'

'Can't you try an ordinary one?' Beckett asked. 'We've got to get the jump on them –'

'No such luck,' Ed said. 'If you'd seen the set up here, you'd know why. Anyway, don't tell Ros I said so, but I always thought electronics could never replace the human touch . . .' he added, knowing that

174

the radio frequency was open to all three of them.

'I heard that,' Ros said. 'Look, I can't believe the laser bug's n.g. – it must be something else.'

'Whatever,' Ed said. 'I'm going in.'

'Okay,' Beckett said. 'Get back to us when you can.'

Ed considered the options. He could, of course, head back round to the front and go in the main entrance – but if they'd laid traps anywhere, that's where they would be. The place was too big for them to have secured it all.

No, there had to be another way.

He ferreted around in his panniers for a moment, then pulled out four metal discs. Each one had a pressure switch and an elasticated strap on one side, and was covered with felt on the reverse.

He glanced up at the dome through the binoculars. Charlesworth and Da Silva appeared to be engrossed in conversation. Quickly, he edged around till one of the lab's towers was between him and the dome. Then he sprinted across the open ground to a spot in the shadow of the wall.

He slipped a disc on each of his hands and feet. Like the laser bug, this was pretty much untested technology. He could only hope it worked better than the bug had.

He pressed one of the discs against the wall. A flip of the switch and it became magnetised. Another flip and the magnetism shut off.

Right, he thought, and started to climb straight up the sheer wall. It took him a couple of moments to get into a rhythm: click on, hand to wall; click foot disc off, move and click to wall; second hand, click off and move and click on; and second foot, click off and move and . . .

He came level with a window, and peered in through

it. Row upon row of gleaming steel tanks, each one, two or three times his height, stretched out in front of him. Nothing moved.

He slipped the disc off his hand and stowed it in his pocket, then tried to raise the window up by its frame.

Nothing doing. He just couldn't get the leverage he needed. He clicked the disc off on the foot nearest the window. Now he was hanging by one hand and foot. His muscles screamed in protest.

He scrabbled to get his knee onto the window-ledge. This is dumb, he thought. This is very, very dumb . . .

He'd tried to teach Beckett the basics of climbing, once. Keep your feet wide, your hands as close as you can to your feet – and above all, keep three points of contact with the rock-face at all times, he'd said.

It was good advice. So why was he spread-eagled against this wall, with his entire weight taken up by two small circles of metal?

Beckett had fallen off the training wall just after Ed had given him that little lecture – fallen onto a nice, soft safety mat. Ed looked down. If he fell, it was fifty feet straight down onto tarmac.

So don't fall, he thought. He got his fingertips round the edge of the window frame and hauled himself up. His knee found the ledge – the sharp metal bit straight through his jeans and cut into him. But that was good. Anything that wasn't a straight plummet to the ground below was good.

Now he was able to get a bit of leverage. The frame still resisted. He snarled at it. Metal squealed and . . . moved.

He cocked his leg over the ledge, turned off the magnetism on the remaining discs and tumbled inside. The gleaming steel tanks cast weird shadows across the floor and walls. Beneath them, CRT monitors and banks of lights and controls glittered in the light from the window.

'All right,' Ed said. 'I'm in – this is one weird place.'

Beckett grunted something in reply.

Ed crept forward, his shoes making no sound on the rubberised floor. Ahead of him, he saw an internal window. A cross-corridor with doors set into the walls. He flattened himself against the last tank and peered round.

No one.

There were windows at either end of the cross-corridor, and what he thought must be more hallways leading off.

The dome had been to his left as he faced the laboratory, and up a level or two. Easy enough, he thought. He took the left arm of the corridor and went as far as he could, ignoring turnings off it. It dead-ended at the window he'd seen.

He backtracked. There were three corridors leading further into the building. He tossed a mental coin and went down the middle one.

More turnings, but still no stairs. He took one, then another. He went through an area that must once have housed airy open-plan offices, but which was now as shadowy and dark as all the rest.

He'd always had a good sense of direction. It was ridiculous to think he might be lost. As far as he could tell, he was now somewhere to the right of the dome, and probably approaching the far side of the laboratory.

Probably.

A turning led off to his right. He glanced down it. There was a door at the end of it; through its window he could clearly see a stairwell.

Good enough.

He headed towards it. The corridor was lined on

either side with heavy steel doors, some with glass observation panels set into them.

Something moved in his peripheral vision. And hadn't he heard a sound?

He jerked round. Nothing. But he knew he had seen something. He backtracked. Now he could definitely hear a faint, irregular thumping.

He stopped and stared around. A trap? He wondered. A cloud passed across the sun, sending shadows leaping across the tiled walls.

Then he spotted it – a flicker of motion from the observation panel in a door far behind him. He ran back.

He peered through the dark glass. All he could make out was the white oval of a face, perhaps a beard and dark hair, or maybe just shadows.

Anyone stuck in this place had to be an enemy of Da Silva's – and surely that made them a friend. He was touching the handle when he thought: unless it's a trap. He had a sudden image of the door opening, of a gun shoved in his face . . . anything.

But he couldn't just walk away.

He stood to the hinge side of the door, reached over and pushed down the handle. Then he pulled the door open a fraction of an inch. It was nearly as awkward as levering the frame up had been, but he managed.

'Okay,' he said. 'Come out slowly, hands in the air – and watch it, I'm armed.' It was a lie, of course. He never carried a gun.

The door edged open a little, then speeded up. A dark-haired figure stumbled out. Ed kicked the door shut. If it came to a fight, at least it would be one on one.

The figure turned. Dark eyes stared at Ed from the pale oval of a face surrounded by a fuzzy beard and hair.

'Charlie?' Ed said, finally recognising Doctor Charles Stross.

'Ed?' The man's voice was little more than a croak. He coughed. 'Sorry,' he said. 'Haven't seen anyone to speak of since I was dumped here.' He ran his tongue over cracked lips. 'He took my prototypes . . . What the hell is going on, Ed?'

Ed glanced around. Standing still made him feel vulnerable. 'No time to explain,' he said. 'I'll show you to the stairs, and I want you to get out of here.' He grabbed Charlie's arm and started dragging him to the end of the corridor. 'My bike's parked near the back of the building. Use my mobile. Get a cab.'

'Okay,' Charlie agreed.

They came to the stairwell doors. Ed motioned to Charlie to stay back. He slipped through the door, ready to take on anything that might be waiting for him.

Nothing.

He looked down the stairwell. The black-enamelled banisters receded into infinity, getting smaller with every turn of the stairs. Nothing moved down there. He peered upwards. Again, the black banisters were stark against the white walls; and again, nothing moved.

Ed slid back into the corridor. 'Okay,' he whispered. 'All clear. If I don't come out in an hour, take the bike and go to Gizmos – Ros and Beckett will know what to do, okay?'

Charlie nodded.

'Well, go on then,' Ed said. 'Straight down two floors – we can't be too far from the front entrance.'

'There's just one thing,' Charlie said. Ed raised his eyebrows at him. 'I've never driven a motorbike before.'

'You'll learn,' Ed said, pushing him through the door.

179

He kept the door open a slit and watched the man disappear down the stairs. He counted to a hundred, then followed him through the door, and went upwards, taking the steps three at a time. One flight up, he passed a window. He glanced out without stopping: a small, black-haired figure was scurrying across the tarmac outside.

Good enough, he thought, and continued on his way.

He was turning the corner from one flight of stairs to the next when the wave of nausea hit him. Something he ate, he decided, and kept climbing.

The world turned in front of his eyes.

He shook his head to clear it. Decided it was a mistake. Yet the world refused to stay still. The steps came up to meet him.

He got his hand out in front of him just in time. Pain jagged through him as all his weight landed on it. Now he could see nothing but a blur of mist, feel nothing but the strangeness of the solid floor turning under him.

He tried to get up. He heaved himself up on to his hands. Dragged himself up a step. Another.

Something black appeared in his field of vision. A foot? He put his hand up to ward it off, but it lashed out and slammed into his chest. He rolled backwards down the stairs and lay helpless at the bottom.

'You see,' Da Silva's voice said. 'Weapons don't have to be lethal – this infra-sound generator works just as well as a bullet. And now we have some insurance.'

The vertigo was beginning to wear off. Ed rubbed his eyes. Two figures were coming down the stairs at him. Da Silva was carrying a pistol with a flaring barrel; he turned round and gave it to Charlesworth, who was just behind him.

'Good,' Charlesworth said. 'Then perhaps we won't have to kill anyone else.'

Da Silva reached down and grabbed Ed by the hair. 'Up you get,' he said. He yanked. Ed grunted, and scrambled to get his feet under him. 'You didn't think I was going to carry you the rest of the way upstairs, did you?'

He switched his grip from Ed's hair to his arm. Ed tried to react, but his legs felt like they were made of rubber. He was too slow – far too slow. Da Silva yanked his arm up behind his back.

'All right, all right,' Ed said. 'I'll walk, okay?'

With his free hand Da Silva reached under his jacket and pulled out a snub-nosed revolver. Its blue-steel surface glinted wickedly in the light. 'This, on the other hand, is lethal,' he said. He jabbed it against Ed's jawbone. 'Especially at point-blank range. Now walk.'

Ed walked.

Ros followed Beckett down the length of the Millennium Metals high-security vault towards the soundproofed R6 chamber. They'd worked hard all afternoon, and she was feeling just a bit smug.

Well, quite a lot smug, actually.

'I've added an additional eight external and six internal surveillance cameras,' she said as she looked around at the place. Metal shelving stretched out as far as her eye could see, all of it stacked high with gold, silver, platinum and other less glamorous but equally valuable metals. If she had anything to do with it, it would all – including the R6 – be staying where it was. 'Also, I've put in heat-sensors and motion-sensors on this floor and the one above.'

Beckett frowned. 'What about the one below?'

For a split second she thought she'd missed something. Then she grinned. 'Funny, Beckett,' she said. 'There isn't one.'

'Just testing.'

They got to the soundproof chamber. She slapped its gleaming titanium door. 'And this is electrified if any unauthorised person gets in here and tries to open it.'

'Nasty,' Beckett said. 'I like it.' He swung open the chamber door, and white light from inside splashed out across his face.

'Well, that's about it,' Ros said. She folded her arms and stared around the vault as if it were all her own work. 'No one alive could get in here and steal the R6 now.'

'I'd say it was completely impossible,' Beckett said.

Ros smiled. She settled back to enjoy a few compliments – she knew she had his complete admiration, but he wasn't exactly free with his praise.

'Because there's no R6 in here to steal,' he said.

He swung the door wide open. The chamber was completely empty.

Keep them talking, Ed thought. Rule number one: they're less likely to do anything sudden if they're too busy thinking up their next reply.

They hadn't taken him up to the dome, but down – right down, Ed guessed, to ground level – to a hangar-like room. The lighting was dim, and came from lamps concealed behind a grid of service conduits.

They stopped at one end of it. In the far distance there was a long foreign-looking car, all sleek curves and flaring tail-fins – not one of the ones Charlesworth and Da Silva had come in. Closer to hand, strange shapes loomed out of the darkness. More tanks, he wondered. Test chambers. They could have been anything.

A cold knot formed in his belly. He thought of Charlie Stross, locked in that cell. Charlie had been lucky. They could lock him in somewhere here, and he'd be nothing but bones before Ros and Beckett found him.

'Guys, can't we talk about this?' he said. Okay, so it wasn't brilliant, but it was the best he could do with the muzzle of a .45 jammed against his ear. 'I mean, what's so special about this R6?'

He didn't think they'd seen him before. Maybe they'd think he was just the hired help.

He swallowed hard. His mouth tasted of copper, and he was having a hard time keeping his breathing steady.

'Quite simply, R6 is unique,' Charlesworth said.

'So you've got a nice little deal with some foreign terrorists?'

Stupid move, Ed, he told himself. Da Silva's eyes went hard with anger.

'You talk too much,' he said. He yanked Ed's headset off and threw it away. It skittered a few feet on the metal floor. 'I'll show you how special R6 is.'

He shoved Ed across the room towards a table. Charlesworth pulled a chair out and put it carefully on a cross which had been marked on the floor with tape. The back of the chair was almost against the wall.

Odd, Ed thought. Very odd.

He licked his lips. 'What now?' he said.

'Sit down,' Da Silva said.

Before Ed could react, his legs were kicked out from under him. He fell backwards, catching his thigh painfully on the arm of the chair.

Charlesworth came forward with a roll of packing tape. Da Silva pushed Ed backwards, and he found himself sitting in the chair.

'Put your arms on the chair's arms,' Da Silva said.

Ed did as he was told. Charlesworth started to bind him to the chair with the tape.

'Hey,' Ed said. 'Do you know how much this leather jacket cost, man?'

Just keep talking. Anything to stop them thinking a

bullet in the brain was the easiest solution.

Meanwhile, he tensed the muscles in his forearms. When he relaxed them, it would make just a bit of slack. Not much maybe, but it was the best he could do.

'Hey, *man*,' Da Silva said, 'I wouldn't worry about the jacket, *capiche*?'

Bad sign, Ed thought. I really want to live to regret the mess you've made of it.

Beckett wasn't a happy man. It was bad enough losing what they'd been hired to protect . . . but losing it to the client was enough to make him spit tacks. He paced the lobby of Millennium Metals, wishing his rubber soles would make a noise on the marble floor. Anything, to help him work off the anger that was raging through him.

Face it, he thought: you don't want Vermeer to have stolen the stuff, because then you have to give up chasing Da Silva, and you *really* want to make sure he gets what's coming to him.

He turned and paced back the other way. Ros sat serenely on one of the leather couches.

She had the sense not to smile at him.

He turned again, paced across the room. Turned.

Ros nodded towards the plate glass window. Georgina Kent's official car drew up outside. Beckett stormed out to it, letting Ros follow.

Despite her bandages, Kent managed to look calm and elegant. She came towards them with the empty sleeve of her coat flapping in the breeze.

'No sign at all of Vermeer?' she asked.

Beckett took a deep breath. He was determined not to lose his temper. 'None,' he said, and realised he was doing a terrible job of not sounding angry. 'He told his staff you gave orders to remove the R6 to a place of safety.'

'Completely untrue,' Kent said. She sounded serene, but now Beckett could see the tension in her face, and the way her good hand was clenching and unclenching.

He took another deep breath. 'Of course,' he said. It really wasn't her fault – and at least she didn't seem to think it was theirs. 'But all the R6 was loaded up and driven away.' He gestured at a silver and gold-coloured Millennium Metals lorry. It was about as inconspicuous as a pink monkey, but then he'd never thought security was Millennium Metals' strong point.

'By Vermeer himself?' Kent asked.

'He took one of the security guards with him,' Ros said.

And that's another point, Beckett thought – we'd better hope for that guard's sake that Vermeer is a lot less ruthless than Charlesworth and chummy boy Da Silva.

Suddenly he was out of patience with the whole lot of them. 'Just tell me one thing,' he demanded. 'Do you think he's working with Charlesworth and Da Silva on this?'

Kent didn't even stop to think about it. 'Unlikely,' she said. 'He and Charlesworth detested each other.'

Beckett stared at the armoured lorry. 'Well, at least he should be easy to spot,' he said. He turned and walked away before Kent could say a thing.

Vermeer watched the streets of the city give way to a multi-lane motorway from the cab of the lorry he had commandeered. It was amazing how much you could see from up here – so much more than when you were walking on the pavement.

In a way, that was the way he felt about his life. He could see it much more clearly now, all the little byways he'd gone down, the blind alleys and dead-end streets. Millennium Metals, for instance: once that had seemed the royal road to success. Not that he had been wrong to think that, but it had become obvious that it was time to take what he could and find a turning off.

He smiled at the image he had created in his mind. Next to him, the security guard he'd brought along to allay suspicions smiled nervously. Poor so-and-so probably thought his job was on the line, whatever he did.

If only you knew, Vermeer thought.

He felt happier than he had in a long time – happier, in fact than at any time since Charlesworth had left Millennium Metals over the development of R6.

Vermeer had been furious then, with a fury which had eaten at his brain and his heart and his happiness. He'd put that down to moral indignation, the white-hot blaze of righteous anger.

An intersection approached. Vermeer looked at the signs, pretending he didn't know where they were going.

'We want the coast road,' he said. It was too firm. 'At least I think we do,' he added.

Now all that fake anger had disappeared. It had gone as if it had never existed, the moment he acknowledged its true cause: envy. He'd been envious at Charlesworth for having the nerve to leave.

Well, envy was just as much a canker as anger; but at least it was simpler to deal with.

Ahead of them was an intersection where layer upon layer of elevated roads crossed and criss-crossed about a knot of tarmac with geometry as complex as the circuitry on the motherboard of any supercomputer. A sign of glowing blue and gold indicated a narrow slipway off it.

'Look,' he said to the guard. 'There's a service station – pull in and we'll get a bite to eat.'

The guard looked worried. 'It's against the rules, Mr Vermeer, sir,' he said.

There was an easy way of dealing with people who were too afraid to act: give them something even nastier to be afraid of.

Vermeer smiled pleasantly enough. 'I wrote the rules,' he said.

He could see from the man's face that he'd put just the right amount of edge into his voice.

The driver hauled on the wheel and the lorry swung smoothly round between an avenue of artificial trees and into the service area. It glided to a stop on one side of a vast swathe of tarmac. Under a wrought iron and plastic canopy, food stalls selling everything from burgers to zabaglione were laid out in a horseshoe around a group of tables and chairs. The place was almost deserted.

Perfect, Vermeer thought.

'I'll get some drinks then, shall I, Mr Vermeer, sir?' said the guard.

'Yes, do,' Vermeer said. He pulled out a couple of notes and shoved them at the man. 'Johnson, isn't it?'

The man shook his head. 'It's Robertson, Mr Vermeer, sir.'

Vermeer suppressed a sigh of impatience. 'Well, get whatever you like, Robertson . . .'

Robertson opened the door, letting a breeze momentarily chill the warm cab. Was it Vermeer's imagination, or could he already smell the sea?

The smell of salt, the smell of freedom . . .

He watched Robertson. The man was staring around the food stalls as if he'd never seen such a choice in his life.

Vermeer hauled himself across into the driver's seat and started the engine. Robertson turned. Vermeer smiled at him and pulled away.

Behind him in the rear-view mirror, he saw Robertson's frantic face. It was almost enough to make up for not having been able to see Kent's when she realised he'd gone.

But he could live without that particular pleasure. He was going to be rich. Filthy, stinking rich.

Ed stared at the glass jar Da Silva was holding. In the bottom of it there was a small lump of silvery metal. All Ed's instincts told him to run. His arms strained at his bonds, and his throat was dry as sandpaper.

'R6,' Da Silva said. 'More discreet than DBX, more powerful even than trisoline. Self-detonating.' He looked Ed straight in the eye. 'There's more than enough here to kill you.'

'You don't say,' Ed said. He might not have fully understood everything Ros had tried to explain about resonant frequencies, but he understood that, all right.

'I'd whisper if I were you,' Da Silva said in an undertone. 'Your voice could set it off.'

Even Ed knew that wasn't true. But he didn't want to provoke Da Silva, so he said nothing more.

Da Silva smiled at him. There was something slow and cruel in that smile, and Ed realised the man was enjoying every moment.

'Get on with it,' Charlesworth said. 'We should be on our way.'

In answer, Da Silva set the flask of R6 down on the table, next to the phone. He pointed along the length of the chamber. 'It seems the previous occupiers had things to protect too,' he said. 'Here we have a move-ment-detector. Once it's activated, if you break the beams –'

'Shhh!' Charlesworth said. Da Silva stopped speak-ing. In the quiet, a tinny female voice could clearly be heard. Ros! Ed thought. 'Someone's trying to contact him,' Charlesworth finished.

He looked around the floor and scooped up Ed's

headset from where Da Silva had thrown it.

'Ed?' Ros said through the headphones. 'Ed, where are you?' There was an odd noise in the background that made it difficult to hear everything she said.

'Damn,' Da Silva said. 'That's the woman. I presume that friend of yours – Beckett, is it? – is still alive too?' A look of fury flashed across his face. 'I should have stuck around and done the job properly.'

'Looks like you aren't such hot stuff after all, Da Silva,' Ed said.

For a moment, he thought Da Silva would hit him. But Charlesworth shushed him again.

Ed could hear Ros's voice even from where he was sitting: 'Ed, I can't hear you, but I assume you can hear me. Vermeer's tricked everyone and made a run for it. We're looking for him now.'

Ed suddenly realised what the noise was – the chuff, chuff, chuff of helicopter rotor blades.

'Vermeer . . .' Charlesworth whispered. He let the headphone dangle by his side.

'You told me he did exactly what the government said,' Da Silva snarled. 'Irreproachable, you said. Unbribeable, you said.'

Charlesworth's face was a blank mask, as if all his dreams had fled from him and left just the broken husk of the man behind. 'I know,' he whispered. 'I never imagined he'd do this . . .'

'Beckett?' Ros said. 'Have you got into traffic control yet?'

Oh no, Ed thought. Not that. He wondered what his chances were of kicking the headset out of Charlesworth's hand. If he'd been standing up, it would have been easy. Sitting down, the chances approached zero. And given that he was also bound, they were somewhere in the negative numbers.

'I don't think I've ever used the phrase "national

interest" so much,' Beckett said. 'And I'll be owing favours till I'm sixty . . .'

He sounded quite cheerful about it though. Ed was glad someone did.

'But you've got what we need?'

'Oh, I've got it all right,' Beckett said. 'Now let's hope it'll help us find Vermeer.'

Charlesworth stood looking at the floor. His arms were folded across his chest, and he was shaking. For a moment, Ed thought he was crying. Then he realised that the man was just barely holding together.

'Pull yourself together,' Da Silva snapped. 'I spent months tracking down the sound-suppressor technology – I'm not giving up now.'

Charlesworth looked up. His face was transfigured by a look of profound hatred. 'He refused to let me market my invention. Now he's stolen it –'

Ed couldn't take the combination of Charlesworth's whining and Da Silva's arrogance. They wanted to think they had him beat, that he was out of the game. Well, he might be out of the game but at least he could show them he wasn't out of everything.

'I thought the R6 was a mistake,' he goaded. Charlesworth whirled on him, watery blue eyes bulging. Go on, Ed thought. Do something. Anything. Make a mistake and let me exploit it. 'An experiment that went wrong – nothing you –'

Charlesworth raised his arm to backhand him across the face. Ed forced himself not to flinch. Before the blow landed, Da Silva grabbed Charlesworth's arm.

'You screwed up over Vermeer,' he said. 'But this man's friends should lead us to him.' Charlesworth pulled his arm away and straightened his jacket. 'You've got the headset?' Da Silva asked. 'Then take the car and meet me outside. I'll attend to this.'

Charlesworth got in the car and drove it straight at

the closed doors. They rose as he approached, then slammed shut after him.

Da Silva walked slowly down the chamber. For all his previous hurry, he seemed to be taking his time now.

He's got something in store for me, Ed thought. Something he hasn't told me about, and he's enjoying it. Sadistic bas –

Da Silva paused in front of one of the pillars that dotted the chamber. He opened a control panel in its side and flicked a switch. A rack bearing what looked like lamps swivelled down out of the ceiling grid. Da Silva flicked another switch. Parallel blue beams of light swept across the chamber from side to side, about six inches off the floor. They stopped just short of Ed's feet.

'Break the beams and the generator produces the exact resonant frequency of that piece of R6,' Da Silva said. 'That tone will be the last thing you ever hear.' He pulled his mobile phone out of its belt-pouch and waved it at Ed. 'Unless you hear the phone.' He smiled his slow, cruel smile. 'I've set the answer machine to play the same tone . . . Insurance, if you like.'

'Come on,' Ed said. He was joking. He had to be joking. 'Anyone could phone – a wrong number, or anything . . .'

Da Silva looked speculatively at his mobile phone. 'Yes,' he said. 'Good, isn't it?'

That's not what I'd call it, Ed thought. Da Silva sighed and put his phone back in its pouch. 'You'd better hope your friends don't try to ring.' He went to a smaller door next to the vehicle exit, opened it, then turned back. 'Bye bye, Ed – and don't break those beams.'

For a moment he was silhouetted against the light. Then he went out. The door slammed shut behind him.

Ed sat alone in the near dark, watching the blue beams slowly rake the floor. And trying not to look at the flask of R6.

Or the phone.

« Thirteen »

Beckett stared round at the banks of television monitors in the Traffic Surveillance headquarters. As he watched, thousands of cars sped by hundreds of video cameras.

The first thing he'd done had been to work out the furthest that Vermeer could possibly have got. Even considering that the man was hardly likely to be flooring the accelerator with all that R6 aboard, it made a depressingly large circle of search.

The computer wall-screen showed it getting larger minute by minute. Unless they got very lucky, their only hope was the computerised pattern-matching program that scanned every vehicle as it passed a camera and compared it with a digitised image of a Millennium Metals van. But the technology was still a bit crude, and it was throwing up a lot of spurious matches.

He stared at the computer, wondering if there was some way of refining the search. The trouble was, if they refined it too much it might just throw away the one match they needed it to make.

'Beckett?' said Ros in his headphones. 'We're following the motorway east from Millennium Metals, but there's no sign of Vermeer so far.' She was shouting, straining to be heard above the roar of the wind and the motor, and the sound of the helicopter's rotor-blades. Kent was with her. Beckett hoped she wasn't going to be too much of a liability if and when things got messy. When Da Silva had raided the Research Annexe, she'd more or less waved her arms at him and yelled, 'Shoot me, shoot me'.

He surveyed the video monitors for a moment, hoping to do what the computers couldn't and give them all a break. 'He hasn't shown up here, either,' he said at last. 'You know, I reckon he might head for the coast – I don't think R6 and aeroplanes are exactly compatible.'

'We'll widen our search pattern in that direction,' Ros said. Beckett heard her talking to Kent.

He stared disconsolately at the banks of monitors. At least she had something to do. It was more than he did.

Just then there was a sharp bleep from the computer. Beckett pushed his chair round. An alert box had come up on the screen: *Match found*.

'Got you!' Beckett said.

'What?' Ros asked.

'Nothing,' Beckett said. 'Probably nothing.'

He tapped commands into the computer. The image on the wall-screen blinked out, and was replaced by a picture of a Millennium Metals van. A caption under-neath gave the number of the camera that was cur-rently picking up the van: *121B 806 – Priority Feed*. As Beckett watched, the picture jumped. When it settled, the camera number had changed.

'Okay,' Beckett said. 'We've got him. He's going east on the motorway . . . just coming up to a roundabout.' He grinned in triumph. 'He's heading south-east –'

'Could be the coast, then,' Ros said. Again, Beckett

heard her say something to Kent. He punched a few extra commands into the system. 'Beckett, lock the pattern-matching program onto the image of the van –'

'I'm ahead of you on that,' he said. Now the computer would track the van as it moved from one camera to the next, and even if they lost it they would be able to pick it up again relatively easily.

'Good,' Ros said. 'Get Traffic Control to patch me into their system and give me a live video feed, also with pattern-matching.'

'I'm on it,' Beckett said. He turned and gestured to the officer in charge.

'And you take to the road,' Ros finished.

Beckett grinned. That was more like it.

Da Silva sprawled back in the passenger seat of Charlesworth's car. They were parked in a lay-by between the laboratory and Millennium Metals. Charlesworth had wanted to keep driving – he'd been sure Vermeer would go home before he left for good, and wanted to start searching from there – but Da Silva had told him to stop.

There was no point running around like rats in a maze when Beckett and his damned friends would do the job for them.

He felt perfectly at ease with the situation: they would find Vermeer and take what they wanted. What Charlesworth thought was rightfully his.

Well, they'd see about that once they were clear of the country.

He looked at Charlesworth. He was such a mouse of a man, scuttling here and there, perpetually scared, perpetually convinced the sky was going to fall on his head.

That was the difference between them, of course: even if Da Silva had been afraid, he wouldn't have let it show. If anything, he would have made sure he seemed relaxed. Not like Charlesworth, who even now was looking out the window, trying to make sure they weren't being followed.

The woman's voice came over the headphones.

'Okay, Beckett,' she said. 'Vermeer's taken the coast road – we've got him now.'

'You got that?' Da Silva said to Charlesworth, who nodded. Charlesworth might be a brilliant scientist, but in Da Silva's opinion he was capable of screwing up the simplest things.

It was a wonder he knew how to drive, Da Silva thought, as they pulled out of the lay-by.

Well, he'd be rid of him soon. And before that, perhaps he'd have a chance to deal with Beckett once and for all.

Ed heaved on the tape that bound him to the chair. There was a bit of play in it, from where he'd tensed his muscles when Charlesworth had bound him.

But not enough.

He couldn't get any leverage at all. He gripped the arms of the chair and tried to push up from his elbows.

Nothing.

Damn, he thought. I really should have done those extra fifty reps in the gym last week.

He stopped. All he was doing was exhausting himself. There had to be another way. What would Ros do? Or Beckett?

He stared around the chamber. The blue beams swept relentlessly across the floor. Beyond them the telephone sat silently on the table next to the jar of R6.

Above them, leading off into the darkness, was a grid of conduits carrying power cables, computer-network fibres and communication lines. Ed had already worked out that they were his escape route . . . if only he could break his bonds.

I'd need to be an escapologist, he thought. And then it hit him.

He leaned back so the chair was braced against the wall, and started to pull his arm out of his jacket. At first he thought it would be just as hard as breaking the tape. Then he got his hand inside the sleeve and managed to grab a bit of lining between his fingers. That gave him enough leverage to move his hand back. Twist his elbow round. He gritted his teeth. Took a deep breath. Got his knee up and pinned the edge of the jacket against the arm of the chair.

He balled his fist and tried to pull it past the constriction of the tape. No dice. He struggled harder, then realised what he was doing.

With a rueful grin he forced himself to relax. He let his hand go limp and pulled . . . and it went straight past the tape.

He jerked down and round, and his arm slid free.

'And with one bound he was free,' he muttered as he twisted round to slip his other arm out of the jacket.

The lining ripped open.

Damn, he thought. He'd *liked* that jacket.

He stood up carefully, taking great care that his feet didn't touch the blue beams. Then he hopped up on to the chair.

His shoulders were sore. He took a moment or two to stretch – there weren't going to be any second chances with what he was going to attempt.

Time, he thought.

He reached up. His hands didn't quite reach the grid. He jumped up and grabbed on, then swung his legs up around the bar.

It creaked ominously, but held.

Ed glanced at the R6. Funny, he thought. The really

dangerous thing on that table wasn't the explosive but the phone.

He looked along the length of the beam. It was going to be a long haul.

Beckett drove as fast as he dared through the heavy traffic. Vermeer had to be somewhere up ahead of him, but it was going to be tough finding him, never mind tailing him.

And anyway, he'd much rather have been going after Da Silva – but it looked like he was going to have to be a problem for another day.

But soon, he hoped. Very soon.

Ros craned out of the chopper window, watching Vermeer's lorry. She grinned, remembering how Beckett's protestations that he should be the one trailing the man, while she stayed back at the Surveillance Centre, had stopped once he realised that going up in a helicopter was part of the plan.

She loved it. In another life, she might have been a pilot, she decided. Except of course, that she would have been a racing driver.

Below her, toy cars and lorries zipped along playset roads. At least the gold and silver Millennium Metals lorry was easy to see.

Just as well. It came to a complicated knot of cloverleaf roundabouts, elevated roads and underpasses.

It disappeared from view.

'Damn,' she muttered.

'Pardon?' Kent asked, in that oh-so-correct accent of hers.

'Nothing,' Ros said. In fact, she'd just spotted the lorry again. 'Beckett? You were right. He's heading for the coast – but not the nearest part. He's gone east by south-east at the next intersection and –'

'Ros?' Beckett said, sounding a bit plaintive. 'Try and get a bug on him, yeah?'

'Okay,' she said. She turned to the pilot – supplied, like the copter, by Kent – and said, 'Take us lower.'

She reached behind her and pulled out a device that looked like a double-barrelled, shoulder-mounted rifle. She fitted the brace to her shoulder and shoved the barrel out of the window, using the edge of the glass for extra support.

The telescopic sight brought the lorry up close. A spot of ruby light appeared just above the second M in Millennium as the laser-sighting system kicked in. Ros breathed out. Squeezed the trigger. A heavy projectile rocketed out of the rifle and impaled itself in the lorry. With luck, Vermeer hadn't felt a thing.

'Gotcha,' Ros said. She brought the rifle back inside and stowed it. 'Okay, Beckett – he's got a bug on board.' She shut the window against the chill of the air, now that there was less need to eyeball the target. 'We'll pull back so as not to scare him,' she said. 'You get in as close as you can.'

'Okay,' Beckett said. There was a pause. 'Excellent – I've got the signal loud and clear.' Ros could just make out the regular beep of Beckett's on-board tracker. 'Have you heard from Ed?' he asked after a moment.

'No,' Ros said. She'd been trying to push that fact to the back of her mind, with some success. But if she was being honest . . . 'I'm getting a bit worried.'

'Oh don't worry about him,' Beckett said. 'He's probably got his feet up somewhere.'

Ed's muscles were screaming agony at him.

He took one hand off the beam. Pain jagged through the arm forced to take the extra weight. He inched forwards, gritting his teeth against the cramps in his thighs. Moved his hand along, and replaced it on the beam.

He took a deep breath. Repeated the whole sequence. Again. And again. Once more for luck, he told himself firmly.

Rested, for a long, blessed moment.

His arms were trembling. He could feel a muscle jumping in his calf.

He had gone up vertical mountains as smooth as polished marble faster than he was traversing this beam.

Still, there was one good thing about the pain. It took his mind off the fear.

He hauled himself a little further. Now he had a problem: he'd come to one of the cross-conduits.

He moved his hands to the other side of it.

No problem, he thought. Now if he just dared . . .

He unwrapped his legs from the conduit. Now he was dangling from his arms, facing back the way he'd come. For a moment, he kept his legs bent up foetal-style. But they hurt so much. And really, the floor was a long way down. Slowly, he let them straighten.

Pain lanced through them. He grunted. Then he started inching his way hand over hand, backwards along the beam. At first it wasn't too bad, but after a few minutes his shoulders started to cramp.

'Definitely – more time in the gym,' he muttered.

He swung his legs up and wrapped them back around the conduit.

Bliss. For now.

He inched forward again.

Something clattered. He shot a terrified glance at the phone, which was now a reassuringly long way away. It wasn't that, though.

He looked around, wondering if Ros and Beckett had managed to track him down. He'd have to warn –

Again, something clattered.

A glint of light on the floor caught his eye. Coins. As

he looked at them, another one fell, dropping neatly between the scything laser beams.

Ed let out a long, ragged breath. It was useless even to pretend he wasn't scared.

A few more coins fell. The beams swept on, undisturbed. Then there was silence.

Ed inched onwards.

Charlesworth brought the car to a halt behind a small boathouse next to a curving sweep of pale green stone that thrust out into the water, forming a semicircle jetty. Moored to it there was a boat: forty silver bullet-shaped feet of seagoing craft. Its solar sails were furled against its mast, and the antenna for its satellite dead-reckoning system was folded flat. Nevertheless, it was clearly well-maintained.

Da Silva opened his door, and was immediately hit by the smell of salt in the air and the freshness of the breeze. The sea lapped against the jetty, its rhythmic lapping interrupted occasionally by the coarse cry of a seagull. In the distance, the marina offices were silhouetted by the setting sun. Da Silva didn't think there would be any trouble from that direction. The place had seemed deserted when they went past it.

'You're certain this is Vermeer's boat?' he asked as they walked across the jetty.

'Oh sure,' Charlesworth said. He pointed to the name etched in the metal of the hull: *Silver Lady*. 'I told you I knew a short-cut to get us here ahead of the crowd. And Vermeer won't be going anywhere else with my invention, I can tell you –' There was an edge of bitterness in his voice.

'It's just business, that's all,' Da Silva said, knowing it would enrage Charlesworth further. The more he thought about it, the more sure he was that there would have to be a parting of the ways fairly soon. Charlesworth was an amateur and a liability. Better to deal with him cleanly.

'If it's just business, why did you leave that bloke to die? We've no quarrel with him.'

'The arms trade is no place for the weak-hearted,' Da Silva said.

'I just want to make money from my invention, not kill people,' Charlesworth said.

Da Silva smiled but didn't speak. There was nothing worth saying to so great a fool.

Ed stared at the rack of beam generators. No matter how far he inched along the bar, it didn't seem to get any closer.

Yes it is, he thought. Yes it is. With an effort he lifted his head and looked back the way he'd come.

Insofar as anything could reassure or cheer him, that did. As far as he could estimate, he was almost there.

'Almost' being a relative term, of course.

Vermeer pulled up next to the jetty. His lovely *Silver Lady* bobbed gently at anchor, waiting for him.

He opened the door of the lorry's cab and climbed out, relishing the taste of brine in the air.

The taste of freedom.

There were a few things he'd have to do to make the *Lady* sea-ready. He decided to leave the R6 where it was until he'd done them.

His shoes slipped a little on the wet surface of the jetty as he walked across to the boat. Soon, he thought, very soon he'd leave all this behind him . . .

A movement on the *Lady* caught his attention. Two figures emerged from beneath the cowling that shielded the companionway that led below.

One was familiar, the other less so.

202

Well, they were just one more problem he was more than capable of dealing with.

'Charlesworth,' he said once he was close enough. 'I knew it was you trying to steal my product.' He looked at the other man: swarthy, coarse-featured – a lout. 'Had to get someone to help you, I see.'

'*My* product,' Charlesworth said. '*My* invention.'

That was just typical of the man – he knew nothing except how to whine. 'The government's, actually,' Vermeer pointed out. 'We were working under licence, remember?'

'So why are you stealing it now?' Charlesworth asked.

'Same as you – to make money,' Vermeer said promptly. Everything was so much clearer now that he'd admitted the truth to himself. It was worth it just to see the shocked look on Charlesworth's face. 'Just that I'm better at making money than you are.'

Charlesworth's mouth trembled. 'You never let me try to market it – you refused.'

'You're too indiscreet,' Vermeer said. 'We'd both be in jail now if you'd had your way.'

Charlesworth swallowed hard. He obviously knew he'd lost. 'Well,' he said. 'We could share it . . . share the money.'

The lout spoke up. 'I don't think so,' he said. He laid a hand on Charlesworth's shoulder.

Charlesworth turned and looked at him with panic-stricken eyes.

But then, Vermeer thought, that was always Charlesworth's problem: being afraid of things.

He smiled at the lout. 'We can arrange something, I'm sure.'

The lout didn't smile back.

Beckett cleared the last of the traffic and floored the

accelerator. A chilly sea-breeze whipped at his face. He wound the window up.

The tracker showed he needed to go east. He took the first turning. The road curved, and then the seashore opened out in front of him.

The Millennium Metals lorry was parked near a boathouse next to a stone jetty, where a boat was moored. He pulled up a little way off, and got out of the car.

He ignored the boat for the time being and went straight to the lorry. There was no one in the cab – no one around at all, in fact. That made him uneasy. Still, he could hear the beating of chopper rotors in the distance, and they were rapidly getting louder.

He yanked open the back doors of the van. A body toppled out at him.

He leapt back just in time. The body crashed to the ground. He bent to turn it over.

Vermeer.

'Well, Mr Beckett,' said a voice he had come to know and loathe. 'It seems you really weren't good enough, after all.' Beckett looked up. Da Silva grinned down at him, but it was the pistol in his hand that grabbed his attention. Da Silva motioned at the chopper, which was circling in to land. 'Shall we wait for your friends? I'd rather not say things twice.'

He jumped down from the van. Beckett had to admit the man was good – the gun never wavered from its target, and there was never a moment when he thought he might be in with a chance of making a break for it.

Da Silva jabbed the gun up into Beckett's jaw. Beckett was facing the van, but he could hear the change in the sound of the chopper's engine as it came in to land.

'Don't be mistaken, Beckett,' Da Silva said. 'One

wrong word, one false move and I *will* blow your head off.'

Beckett heard footsteps on the stone behind him. Two sets of footsteps, he corrected himself. He schooled himself not to move.

'Oh well done, Beckett,' Ros said.

'Yeah,' Beckett said, moving his mouth as little as possible, and watched her expression change.

'You've really done very well so far,' Da Silva said. Condescending bastard, Beckett thought. 'But I'm afraid you go no further. I've got buyers lined up for this material, and they're not the sort of people you can disappoint.'

'I don't want to seem obvious,' Ros said, 'but what makes you think we won't try to stop you?'

'Ros, I –' Beckett started. Da Silva jabbed the barrel of the pistol hard into his jaw. He shut up.

Da Silva pulled a mobile phone out of his pocket with his free hand. 'Your colleague is currently languishing in a . . . safe place, unable to move. Near him is a quantity of R6, ready to explode when the correct tone is played from the telephone answering machine.' He smiled. In that moment Beckett realised his hatred for the man went past anything personal. Before, he'd wanted to be the one to bring him down. After this, he didn't care how it happened. Just so long as it happened. 'Unless you help us get safely away, I'll have no hesitation in dialling the number and blowing him up.'

'It's a bluff,' Kent said from somewhere outside Beckett's rather limited field of view.

'It's not,' Charlesworth said. 'He means it.' He sounded scared. Maybe he'd realised he was playing with the big boys now, Beckett thought.

It was a little bit late for that.

Da Silva slowly pulled the gun away from Beckett's face. He turned the hand holding the mobile phone and revealed that he was holding something else.

Beckett stared at the tangle of wire, appalled. 'Yeah,' he said, struggling to keep his voice steady. 'That's Ed's headset, but how do we know the rest is true?'

But he thought of Vermeer lying dead nearby, and the way that Wallace had stared blindly up at him, and he knew that it was.

'It is,' Charlesworth said frantically. 'He killed Vermeer and he'll kill your friend.'

'Getting squeamish?' Da Silva asked. 'You wanted to make money out of an explosive. Explosives kill people.'

'But Vermeer is dead,' Charlesworth said. 'I could take over the company. Sell the R6 legitimately.'

And it would still kill people, Beckett thought. Only the identity of the killers would change.

'Don't be stupid,' Da Silva said. He started to punch a number into the phone. When he was done, he turned it so they could all see the number on the LCD display. It could be the number of the speaking clock in some tinpot little country on the other side of the world, Beckett thought: but Da Silva had them and he knew it. They didn't dare take any chances with Ed's life at stake. 'Now,' Da Silva went on, 'I only have to press the "send" button to connect the call.' He levelled the pistol at Beckett. 'So do as I say.'

Ros nodded.

After a moment, so did Beckett.

Freedom!

Ed shimmied past the rack of beam generators. The switch was beyond his reach.

Six inches more.

Done.

He dropped to the floor and landed heavily. For a moment he lay there, winded. Then he got up and limped over to the door. There was a small window set into it, but there was no way Ed would be able to get through it. Besides, he was sure it would be reinforced.

He tried the door. It was locked. He stared at it in frustration for a moment, then remembered his electronic lockpick.

And it was in his jacket pocket. He glanced back down the chamber. It couldn't have been more than a hundred feet. It might as well have been as many miles.

'Just have to do it the old-fashioned way,' he muttered to himself.

Fine idea, he thought – but even the old-fashioned approach needed something to use as a lockpick. He searched his jeans' pockets. Nothing.

He looked desperately around him. The place was pristine.

Beckett slid the case of R6 into the boot of Da Silva's car. Ros put hers next to it.

'Back off,' Da Silva said. He stepped towards them, brandishing the pistol. 'You with the bandage – close the boot.'

Kent stepped forward and slammed it down. Da Silva backed towards the driver's side door. The gun never wavered. With his other hand, he opened the door.

Beckett lunged forward. 'What about Ed?' he demanded.

'Want to speak to him?' Da Silva asked. He held up the phone. 'Let's call him.' He pressed the 'send' button.

The phone rang.

Ed looked round, panic-sticken. There was nothing

he could use as a lockpick. He slammed his hand into the window. Tried again, harder. He could take a few lacerations . . .

It still didn't work. He stood off, and kicked the window as hard as he could.

Nothing.

'Damned reinforced glass,' he muttered.

Beckett threw himself at the man. Even so, he wasn't fast enough. Charlesworth got there first.

For a moment, they struggled. Da Silva held the phone up out of Charlesworth's reach. He leapt for it. Da Silva tried to knock him away. He failed. Charlesworth grabbed his arm. Da Silva hauled back and threw the phone as hard as he could.

It arced through the air and landed on the upper deck of the boat.

Ros raced after it. Beckett was momentarily distracted. When he looked back, the gun was on the floor. Someone – maybe Charlesworth – kicked it.

It skittered across the ground. Charlesworth dived for it. Beckett lunged at Da Silva.

'Not good enough, huh?' Beckett snarled. 'Well, how good is this, pal?' He landed one good punch in Da Silva's midriff.

He tried for another. Da Silva straight-armed him out of the way. He staggered back. It only took a split second for him to get his balance, but it was too late.

Da Silva was running towards Charlesworth, who was holding out the gun as if it might go off if he breathed wrong.

'Don't come near me,' he said.

'You won't shoot me,' Da Silva said. He continued walking towards Charlesworth. 'I'm your only hope.' He was very close now. 'Besides, you don't have the balls.'

Something in Charlesworth's eyes alerted Beckett. He sprinted across towards Da Silva. 'Don't,' he shouted.

Da Silva reached for the gun.

There was a muffled bang. Da Silva's body slumped to the ground. Crimson trickled from his mouth.

'I didn't mean to . . .' Charlesworth whimpered.

'No,' Beckett said. 'I don't suppose you did.'

The phone stopped ringing. The answerphone kicked in.

'Bad luck, Ed,' Da Silva's voice said. 'It looks like someone wants to talk to you –' Ed looked wildly around. There was no escape, nowhere to run. He ran anyway. One of the tanks blocked his way. 'So here, as promised, is the tone R6 loves to hear.' Inside, Ed thought. My only hope. He yanked open the door and climbed in.

'Bye bye, Ed,' Da Silva's voice said.

Ed pulled the door shut, leaving just the tiniest crack so he could open it again. Only a thin stream of light filtering through the observation panel lightened the darkness.

A single, pure note shrilled out.

The world erupted. Thunder roared out, and the light turned orange. The tank ripped free of its moorings and careened through the air. Ed got his free hand up in front of his face and curled into a foetal position.

The tank slammed into something. Ed's head whipped back and cracked against bare metal.

The world went dark around him.

Beckett stared at Ros as she clambered down off the boat. She had Da Silva's phone in her hand. Beckett could tell from her expression that it wasn't good news.

'There's nothing,' she said when she got to them. Her voice was heavy with grief.

Charlesworth held Da Silva's gun out, butt-first, to Beckett. 'I'm sorry about your friend,' he said.

Beckett grabbed the gun. Then he grabbed Charlesworth. All the rage of the past few days – the beating, the taunting by Da Silva, the attempt on his and Ros's life, and above all the murder of Ed – rose up inside him in an unstoppable red tide. 'You're *sorry*?' he said. He jammed the gun up against Charlesworth's neck. The smaller man's eyes went wide with terror. 'Well, you ain't as sorry as you're going to be.'

'Beckett!' Ros said. He wouldn't look at her. If he looked at her, he might lose control altogether. 'Beckett, it isn't worth it . . .'

Beckett turned to her. 'Oh no?' he said. It was all he could do to stop his finger tightening on the trigger.

Ed came to in a haze of pain. It was so dark . . .

He raised his hand to the back of his head and felt a trickle of blood.

That was it: the R6 had gone off.

He searched around and found the door. He pushed it open and stumbled out.

The laboratory was a charred wreck. Smoke caught at the back of his throat. Daylight poured through a huge gash in the wall. Small fires burned here and there. There was a scream of tearing metal, and a joist broke free.

He stumbled towards the light. Fresh air had never tasted so sweet. He found his motorbike in the alley and sat slumped astride it.

After a moment it occurred to him that he hadn't checked in for hours. It felt like hours anyway. He took a phone from the bike's pannier and dialled Beckett's number.

'Beckett,' he said. 'I hope I haven't missed all the fun. I've been a bit tied up.'

Beckett didn't answer him. He just said, 'Ros? It's for you.'

But what Ed couldn't understand was why Beckett sounded so pleased.

Beckett handed the phone to Ros.

'Hello,' she said hesitantly.

'Hi,' Ed said. 'I think someone left the gas on here.'

She smiled rapturously, and Beckett found himself doing the same.

She turned to Charlesworth. 'Aren't you the lucky boy then?' she said.

Beckett turned away. He suddenly realised he wasn't the only one who might have done something stupid that afternoon: just the first in the queue.

He walked over to Da Silva's body. The man's blind eyes stared up at him.

'I guess in the end you just weren't good enough, *pal*,' he said.

BUGS – The TV Series

This book is based on two episodes of the TV series BUGS: 'Hot Metal' written by Alan Whiting from a story by Brian Clemens, and 'Manna From Heaven' written by Gregory Evans. These episodes were first broadcast on BBC1 on 20 May and 27 May 1995. They were directed by Ken Grieve and Brian Farnham respectively.

Producer – Brian Eastman
Co-Producer – Stuart Doughty
Production Designers – Rob Harris and Mark Raggett
Series Consultant – Brian Clemens
Script Consultant – Colin Brake
Executive Producer for the BBC – Caroline Oulton

BUGS is a Carnival Films production.

Read the full story in Virgin's non-stop action novels

Available from all good book shops!